HOMICIDE:

THE NOVEL

JEROME PREISLER

BOULEVARD BOOKS, NEW YORK

HOMICIDE: THE NOVEL

A Boulevard Book / published by arrangement with
National Broadcasting Company, Inc.

PRINTING HISTORY
Boulevard edition / November 1996

The Putnam Berkley World Wide Web site address is
http://www.berkley.com/berkley

ISBN: 1-57297-227-0

BOULEVARD
Boulevard Books are published by The Berkley Publishing Group,
200 Madison Avenue, New York, New York 10016.
BOULEVARD and its logo are trademarks
belonging to Berkley Publishing Corporation.

PRINTED IN THE UNITED STATES OF AMERICA

10 9 8 7 6 5 4 3 2 1

For Suzanne
and this time
also for Charlene, Noni and Jones . . .
wonderful ladies and inspirations to me, all.

AUTHOR'S NOTE

I would like to thank some folks who have made working on this project an exceptional pleasure: the ever-supportive Elizabeth Beier, Tom Fontana (who is both heart and soul of the TV series upon which my novel is based) and his crack assistant Sean Jablonski at SL/TMF Productions, and last but far from least, my agent and friend Fran Lebowitz.

In this book, the historical and cultural information presented about the Romany is accurate (at least from the perspective of a non-Gypsy author) except in a few minor instances, where I have intentionally fudged for dramatic purposes. And while I'm making excuses, a word of advice to you, kind reader—don't try using my geography to find your way around Baltimore. Trust me, you'll get hopelessly lost.

HOMICIDE:

THE NOVEL

ONE

AFTER NEARLY A decade in Homicide, the thing that always struck Frank Pembleton when he first arrived at a murder scene was not the human and material wreckage, not the spilled blood or the heavy reek of death, not the physical horror and violence of the crime that had been committed, but the sheer waste of it, the ruined possibilities, the trashed hopes and dreams, the sense that all the intangible yet vital elements of a life cut short were dissipating in the air around him like smoke from a doused flame . . . or *flames* in the case of double murder, such as he now had on his hands. Sometimes that feeling of waste crept into his pores and became a hollowness that wouldn't let him sleep, but at those times he would keep in mind how privileged he was doing the job that he did, seeking the truth, pursuing justice for those who could no longer act for themselves. And he would remember that the alternative was to let it become routine,

1

lump the victims together the way they did in crime stats or front-page headlines, which, for a detective, was the beginning of the end.

Of course, some days *were* tougher than others.

"Even a man who is pure of heart and says his prayers by night . . ."

Pembleton looked at Detective John Munch, with whom he'd gotten stuck this morning because his regular partner, Tim Bayliss, had traded shifts with Kay Howard, who'd switched with yet a fourth member of the squad who had taken a few days off to settle some personal affairs. A thin, hawkish man in a charcoal-gray suit and tinted wire glasses, Munch looked more like an ambulance chaser than a cop as he studied the two corpses on the floor of the Gypsy parlor.

"What was what?" Pembleton said.

"What was what?"

"What you just said."

"Oh," Munch contemplatively tugged on his lapel. "Haven't you ever seen *The Wolfman*? You know, Lon Chaney?"

Here we go, Pembleton thought, reaching into a pocket for his cigarettes. He'd chosen a hell of a week to try cutting back on his tobacco habit.

"When I was ten years old," he said. "Maybe eleven."

"Never since?"

Pembleton shook his head. He felt like a mouse chasing after a dangled piece of cheese.

"A real shame," Munch said. "Because it was a Gypsy curse that turned Chaney into a werewolf."

"And I assume this has something to do with what happened to these vics."

"Well, they're Gypsies, aren't they?"

Pembleton fired up his disposable lighter and held it to the tip of his cigarette.

Yes, Gypsies they had been.

Past tense.

Taking a drag off his smoke, he looked around the back room of the fortune-telling joint, which more properly might have been considered a psychic emporium, or maybe a telepathic boutique, given its upscale decor, and the variety of services it provided. This was a far cry from the traditional open-anytime *ofisas* with their folding tables, grimy crystal balls and tattered palmistry charts. Here the regular office hours were posted out front on a fluorescent message sign, and the high-tech crystal ball in the parlor generated flashes of pale blue lightning in its depths, with "CLAIRVOYANT" printed in slick contemporary lettering on the awning above the display window, and the window itself bordered by electric blue neon tubing, and festooned with multicolored neon stars and planets and crescent moons, as well as neon signs advertising ESP, tarot and dream readings, astrological, numerological and phrenological consultations and many other occult specialties.

"So Chaney goes to the Gypsy camp, I don't know why," Munch was saying. "Could be to ask the fortune-teller whether this woman he loves feels the same way about him, or wants to have sex with him that night. The reason isn't important, because it's what happens afterward that gets him zapped by the curse."

"Uh-huh," Pembleton said absently.

He gazed out the window at the street, where a pretty woman in a black beret was brushing snow off the window of her car, and a rachitic Old English sheepdog was staggering over a high drift as its owner knelt to brace its weakened hindquarters, and shopkeepers were digging narrow paths from the curb to their doors, their shovels scraping harshly against frozen concrete. It was late November, just a week after Pembleton's newborn daughter had celebrated her first Thanksgiving, and earlier that morning he'd noticed the wonderful smell of Mary's turkey lingering faintly in their kitchen, and looked out the window to discover that winter had roared in with a vengeance overnight, burying Charm City under six inches of snow.

Munch was still jabbering about his monster movie.

". . . walking home through the woods when he gets attacked by a werewolf, and beats it to death with the silver handle of his cane, and the werewolf reverts to human form, and turns out to be the fortune-teller's son . . . or husband—it's been a while since I've seen the flick myself."

"And so he curses Chaney with his dying breath,

4

and Chaney becomes a werewolf," the medical examiner piped in.

A pear-shaped guy named Scheiner, he was crouching over the body of the female victim, whose face and head were dotted with little red bullet holes. The male sprawled across the room from her had caught several slugs in the chest.

"You hit the buzzer too soon," Munch said, sounding like Alex Trebec. "He didn't have to *verbally* curse him—all it took was a good bite. You could say the werewolf disease is like rabies in the way it's transmitted."

"Whatever," Scheiner said. "One thing I can tell you for sure, these two were offed by a ten-mil semiauto, not some Gypsy curse."

"I suppose," Munch said. His eyes took in a litter of broken teacups near an overturned table to his right, passed over the blood-spattered surface of an ornately framed wall mirror and settled briefly on an astrological circle hanging on the opposite wall. The zodiac signs on the chart looked like hiero-glyphic characters and had Egyptian names—Isis replacing Virgo, Ichton instead of Pisces, Anubis for Capricorn.

"You *suppose*?" Pembleton asked incredulously.

Munch ignored him.

"What the hell's a phrenological consultation anyway?" he said to nobody in particular.

"Phrenology's the study of the head," offered one of the four crime scene techs scouring the room for evidence.

"Close, but no cigar," the ME said. "Just look at the Greek root of the word."

Pembleton frowned. Now Scheiner was trying to be a game show host.

"There's *phren,* meaning 'mind,' and *logos,* science. We're talking about the *mind,* not the head."

"That's a difference?" the tech said.

"Hey, we're supposed to be educated guys here."

"I thought *psychology* was the science of the mind," Munch said.

"For my two cents, psychology's more of a discipline than a science," the ME said.

He carried his kit from the woman's corpse to the dead man, avoiding a puddle of blood as he stooped over him.

"By the way," he said, "since there's a slight rigor present in both bodies, I'm guessing they've been dead for several hours. Also, the guy's got a lot of contusions and abrasions."

"He fought with the killer," Pembleton said.

"And how," Scheiner said.

"So tell me about phrenology," Munch said.

"It's a load of bullshit," Scheiner said. "*Pseudo-*science. Supposed to gauge character and mental capacity by the size, shape and appearance of the skull. Nineteenth-century researchers were big on it. The Nazi quack doctors too, for that matter. Crazy bastards would go around measuring people's skulls with calipers to find out whether they had *Übermensch* potential in their genes."

Pembleton unconsciously rubbed his shaved scalp.

He was still thinking about the bruises on the dead man's body, and how he'd fiercely grappled with whoever had taken his life. There were signs of that struggle everywhere in the room: toppled furniture, scattered baskets and baubles, a litter of broken glass and china—gouges on the walls from wild shots.

What else to help reconstruct what happened?

The jamb of the entry door was splintered and nicked around the lock plate; it had obviously been jimmied open with a crowbar. So the killer had broken into the place, passed through the parlor without disturbing a thing and entered the back room. Judging from the mess, he'd gotten there before the victims and been caught by surprise, which probably meant his original intention hadn't been to commit murder.

Pembleton strode around the room, looking for more pieces of the puzzle. A tall black man in his mid-thirties, he moved with the light-footed grace of a dancer, and had the sort of striking, if not conventionally handsome, looks that always drew second glances on the street. All contained energy, his almost Zenlike outer calm housed a forceful, occasionally volatile core. Today he was wearing an eggshell Burberry trench coat and wide-brimmed fedora. The hat—which he'd taken off because of the stifling warmth inside the fortune-telling joint— was what some people called his trademark, a characterization he disliked but didn't waste time resisting.

He noticed a small, bunched-up rug under a corner table and carefully nudged it aside with his foot.

His brow suddenly furrowed with concentration.

"Munch," he said, kneeling to inspect the area that had been covered by the rug. "Check this out."

Munch squatted down beside him.

On the exposed floorboards were the remnants of four evenly spaced metal bolts and a scattering of metal filings.

"Floor safe," Munch said. "Somebody used a hacksaw to cut the bolts."

"Why bother cracking the lock when you can walk off with the whole kit and caboodle?" Pembleton said.

"Could've been a fortune stashed away back here," Munch said. "Gypsies don't keep their savings in banks."

Pembleton looked at him. "Is that a fact?"

Munch nodded.

"A *fact*?"

Munch nodded again. "Their gains are too ill-gotten. And they don't trust big establishments."

"I didn't realize you were an expert," Pembleton said.

"I'm not. But everybody knows about Gypsies and banks."

Pembleton blinked.

"I say something wrong?"

Pembleton rose without answering him and turned toward the parlor.

It was now eight-thirty A.M. The victims had been found two hours earlier by a man named Mihial Bash, who'd been vague about whether he actually operated the fortune-telling joint, yet was clear about the fact that he *rented* the storefront space and resided in the apartment above it, which to Pembleton seemed a distinction without a difference. Bash claimed to have been returning from a visit with relatives when he'd found the street entrance wide open, gone inside to investigate and almost tripped over the bullet-riddled corpses of his nephew and his nephew's wife, whom he'd identified as Alexei and Christine Bash. Upon making his terrible discovery, Mihial had rushed to call the police, waited for a squad car to show up and given the patrolmen his account of what happened.

He was now in the parlor with those same responding blues, looking pulverized with shock.

Pembleton went in to speak to him.

Dressed in a black leather jacket, dungarees and a bright red silk neckerchief, Bash was a dark-haired, brown-skinned, thick-set man of about fifty. He sat on a fan-backed wicker chair beside the table that supported the crystal ball, the top of his head almost brushing against the bottom of a knickknack shelf with pigeonholes full of trinkets and religious statuettes.

"Sir, I have a few questions," Pembleton said, taking out his pad and pencil.

Bash looked up at him with blank eyes. He was

9

clenching a large gold amulet in his right hand and nervously twisting its chain around his left.

"You mentioned that you were out all night with relatives. Could you tell me specifically what you were doing?"

"Playing cards," he said. "At their apartment."

"And the names of the family members you were visiting . . . ?"

"I already gave 'em to the other cops," Bash said, and jabbed his chin at one of the blues who'd answered the 911.

"You were alone when you got back here this morning?"

"Yeah."

"Anybody upstairs?"

"My mother. And my daughter Lovera."

"And neither of them heard anything unusual . . . ?"

"Old lady's going deaf. Her ears might as well be wood."

"What about Lovera?"

"She likes to be called Vera. And she wasn't here."

"Mr. Bash, you just told me—"

"I told you my daughter was upstairs *now*." Bash's expression had become sullen. "You didn't say you meant last night."

Pembleton looked at him.

"Does Vera live with you?"

"No."

"So it's just your mother and you."

"Vera's a grown woman. Got her own mind," Bash said irritably. "She doesn't have to stay with her family."

Pembleton wondered why Bash had gotten so ruffled at the mention of his daughter, and made a follow-up notation in his pad.

"Sir, can you tell me what your niece and nephew were doing here this morning?"

"I dunno. Probably just visiting."

Pembleton raised his eyebrows.

"While *you* happened to be out visiting other members of your family," he said.

"Why not?"

"At six o'clock in the morning."

"Like I said, why not?"

"It seems like an odd hour to be paying someone a house call—"

"Maybe to a *gajo*—"

"A what?"

"A *gajo*," Bash repeated.

"He means a non-Gypsy." This from Munch, who had come in from the other room and was standing next to Pembleton. "It's a slightly pejorative term."

Pembleton hesitated. As an African-American, never mind an African-American who was a cop—which made him the Man to many of his so-called brothers on the street—he'd believed he had endured every racial epithet that could be flung at him, but here was a new one to try on for size. One that

11

lumped him in with the majority of the population, no less.

"Bullshit," Bash said.

"Excuse me?" Pembleton said.

"I ain't callin' anybody names. But a *gajo*'s a *gajo*. We got different ways of seeing things, is all."

Pembleton sighed. "Let me get this straight, Mr. Bash. Your niece and nephew arrived before sunrise to pay you a visit, by coincidence picking a night on which *you* happened to be out playing cards with some other relatives."

"That's right. Second cousins on my mother's side."

"And what about the safe?" Munch asked, changing tacks to throw Bash off balance.

Pembleton instantly recognized what he was doing and let him have the ball. He might be a pain in the ass, but he was also a damned good detective.

Bash remained stonefaced.

"What safe?" he asked.

"The one that's missing from the back room," Munch said.

"I don't know what the hell you're talking about," Bash said.

"Mr. Bash, there are cut bolts on the floor of the type that are normally used to secure a safe."

Bash shrugged. "Never noticed them. Maybe you oughtta talk to the person who rented this place before me."

"You're saying the bolts were there when you moved in?"

"I'm saying maybe."

"And you've been here *how* long?"

"Gonna be five years in January."

Munch exchanged glances with Pembleton but didn't mention the metal filings they'd found under the crumpled rug.

"One last thing, Mr. Bash," Pembleton said. "Can you tell us—"

"Look, what do you want from me? Those two dead people back there are my *family*—"

"I understand, sir, and would just like to know whether you have any ideas about who might have wanted to harm them," Pembleton said. "Or yourself for that matter, since the shooting occurred on your premises."

Bash's black eyes sharpened, and the hand in which he was holding the amulet tightened into a white-knuckled fist.

"Yeah," he said without hesitation. "Matter of fact, I know exactly who did it."

Pembleton leaned closer, his eyes widening with surprise.

"You *know* . . . ?"

"It's the fucking Demetros."

"The what?"

"The *Demetro* clan. Gotta be them. They been tryin' to pick us off for almost thirty years."

"Hold on a minute," Pembleton said. "You're telling me an entire *clan* of people might have had some motive to—"

"The whole worthless bunch," Bash said. "Their

13

headman put an *armaya* on me, did it right to my face."

"An ar-*what*?" Munch asked.

"*Armaya*," Bash said. "A curse."

Pembleton looked at Munch.

Munch looked back at him.

"Told you so," he said.

TWO

"*YEKKA BULIASA NASHTI beshes pe done grastende.*"

"My grandmother says that with one behind you cannot sit on two horses."

Neither Pembleton nor Munch had the foggiest notion what that was supposed to mean, or how it related to the question they'd just asked, which was simply whether Mihial Bash's elderly mother, Betshi, had heard any unusual noises downstairs in the early hours of the morning. They were in the apartment above the fortune-telling joint, trying to get whatever information they could out of Betshi, who was thus far the only potential witness to the murders they were investigating. But if Betshi spoke a word of English, she was doing a great job of pretending otherwise, leaving Vera Bash to act as interpreter for the cops.

Pembleton rubbed the back of his neck. "Ma'am, perhaps I wasn't making myself understood—"

"*Stanki nashti arakenpe manushen shai,*" Betshi

Bash said, her withered fingers playing with the shawl on her lap. White-haired, gap-toothed and wearing a shapeless floral peasant dress, she had a face like dusty cobwebs and was a ringer for the fortune-teller whose lycanthropic son had sicced Lon Chaney in the old horror flick Munch had been thinking about for hours now.

"My grandmother says that mountains do not meet, but people do."

Pembleton looked at Vera Bash in frustration.

"Grandma can be a little dense," she said, shrugging.

"Ma'am," Munch said. "If you could just get it across that my partner and I—"

"Vera."

"Excuse me?"

"Please call me Vera."

Munch nodded, thinking he would call her anything she asked, not to mention strip down to his boxers and do a chicken dance if that was what she wanted, namely because she was so mesmerizingly gorgeous she could have been a fashion model or a Hollywood actress. Slender, leggy and in her late twenties, she had hair like midnight, eyes like moonlight, and wore a man's white shirt and black high-heeled boots over a pair of blue jeans that were snug as a second skin.

"Vera," Munch said. "We realize there's a communication problem here—"

"*Tell* me about it. I grew up in this family." She smiled thinly and brushed a fringe of jet-black hair from her cheek, silver bangles tinkling on her wrists, silver pendant swaying on a silver chain around her neck.

Munch noticed that her teeth were perfectly white and even.

"Uh . . . right," he said, clearing his throat. "Still, we're interested in anything she can tell us about what happened downstairs or what she might have been doing *when* it happened."

"For instance," Pembleton said, "was she asleep or awake at about six o'clock this morn—"

"*Kon del tut o nai shai dela tut wi o vast,*" Betshi Bash said, popping her thin, wrinkled lips.

"She says that he who willingly gives you one finger will also give you the whole hand," Vera told Munch.

Pembleton sighed.

"Miss Bash . . . Vera . . . would anyone mind if I smoked?" he asked.

"Go ahead," Vera said. "Grandma'll probably want to bum off you, though."

He reached for his cigarettes, shook one from the pack and offered the pack to the old woman, who eagerly snatched it from his hand. She took out four cigarettes, slipping three underneath the shawl on her lap and the fourth into her gummy mouth. Then she returned what was left of the pack to Pembleton without thanking him, reached for a matchbook on a nearby table and lit up.

"Just out of curiosity, does your grandmother understand *anything* we say?" Munch asked.

"Practically everything," Vera said. "But like I told you, she's thick. Always has been. Thinks anything except Romany is going to make her tongue rot."

"Romany . . . ?"

"We Gypsies call ourselves *Rom*—that just means 'Man'—and our traditional language *Romany*. It's kind of like Sanskrit, except there's no written form."

"Oh."

"Part of the work I've been doing at school is to preserve it and codify a standardized grammar."

"You're a student?"

She smiled a little. "I'm with the anthropology department at Georgetown. Took a couple of semesters off from teaching to get my project funded and rolling."

"Oh." Munch's mouth felt dry. Beautiful and brainy. A *college professor*. He was having trouble recalling what the hell he'd started off asking her.

"Georgetown University's quite a hop away," Pembleton said. "I take it you don't live in Baltimore."

"Haven't for over a decade. My parents couldn't cope with the fact that I wanted an education, something they believed was worthless and corruptive. It threatened them, made them feel I was turning my back on our customs, shunning the old ways to join the *gaje* world. And embarrassing them in front of the rest of the clan."

"So you got in hot water with Mom and Dad

because you *didn't want* to play hookey," Munch said. "Did they also punish you when you ate your veggies and brushed before going to bed?"

She smiled fleetingly. "In Gypsy society a woman's role is supposed to be having kids and making money for the men to gamble away. Even when you're a little girl they have you out on the street selling carnations. I left home as soon as I legally could, pretty much cut off ties with the family for a long time."

"You know, my father once stole a year's worth of my saved allowances and bet it all on his favorite horse at the track," Munch said.

"No kidding?" Vera gave him a dubious look.

"Really," Munch said. "He—"

"*Feri ando payi sitsholpe te nayuas,*" Betshi Bash interrupted.

"What'd she say?" Pembleton asked.

"It is in the water that one learns to swim."

Pembleton exhaled impatiently and leveled a penetrating glance at Vera.

"About Christine and Alexei," he said. "How exactly were they related to you?"

"Alexei was a second cousin," she said. "My father's uncle's son."

"And would you know why anyone would have wanted to harm them?"

"We really didn't have much contact," she said, shaking her head. "Not since I was a kid, anyway."

"Does the name Demetro mean anything to you?"

19

"Sure." She shrugged. "They're another clan in the area."

"Your father believes they may have been involved in the shootings."

"Sounds familiar. He probably also blames the Demetros for the snow that fell last night. And the last time he got a parking ticket. And his arthritis." She paused, sighed. "Detective Pembleton, tribal rivalries are practically a tradition among the Rom. The conflict gets their juices flowing. But they almost never go beyond hurling accusations at each other."

"Almost?"

She crossed her arms and shrugged.

Pembleton exhaled a stream of smoke through his nose. "Miss Bash . . . I'm sorry, it *is* Miss, isn't it?"

She nodded affirmatively and Munch felt his stomach flutter.

"Miss Bash, you said that you're in the middle of an academic project. . . ."

"That's right."

"And that you weren't close to the deceased."

"Yes."

"So if you'll pardon my asking, what are you doing in town?" Pembleton asked.

"My father telephoned me early this morning," she said. "Right after he found the bodies. As you can imagine, he was very upset, so I drove in to keep him company."

"I assume he had more of an active relationship

20

with Alexei and Christine than you did," Pembleton said.

"Sure," she said. "They lived within five or six blocks of each other. Strangers in a strange land."

There was a long silence. Pembleton smoked his cigarette and watched the old lady watching him.

"Talk to your grandmother, after we leave," he said flatly. "If she knows anything, she'll have to tell us sooner or later."

"Mashkar le gajende leski shib si le Romeski zor," she said, and suddenly pointed a skeletal finger at him.

He waited for Vera to translate but this time she said nothing.

"Miss Bash . . . ?" he prompted.

"Grandmother said that, surrounded by *gaje,* the Rom's tongue is her only defense."

Pembleton stood there a moment, then flipped his notepad shut.

"She *will* have talk to us," he said at last, returning the pad to his pocket and handing Vera Bash his business card. "Give me a call if you think of anything that may be relevant to our investigation."

Vera nodded, stood up and opened the door for the detectives.

"Thank you," Pembleton said, and turned into the outer hallway.

Munch lingered behind him a moment. Started to ask her the question that had been on the tip of his tongue for the past fifteen minutes.

Hesitated.

"Yes, Detective?" she said.

He took a deep breath and forced out the words.

"I was wondering," he said, "if you'd like to have dinner with me this weekend?"

Vera looked at him with her striking brown eyes and smiled.

"Will you promise to finish telling me about your stolen allowance?"

"I do solemnly swear," he said, his stomach still fluttering like a schoolboy's.

"Then you're on," she said.

THREE

FRANK PEMBLETON'S FIRST Rule of Detection: in any murder investigation, you start out by doing your basic legwork. This means carefully looking at the crime scene and talking to the person who discovered the body, as well as everyone present who knew the victim and might be able to tell you when he was last seen alive. Then you work the street, knocking on doors and interviewing neighbors, bearing in mind that, nine times out of ten, a person who's seen anything out of the ordinary would rather crawl into a shell than voluntarily come forward with information.

The meat wagon was arriving as Pembleton and Munch stepped out onto the sidewalk to begin their canvas; silent as the death its presence betokened, it nosed past the police cruiser parked across the intersection to divert civilian traffic, moved slowly up the street toward the *ofisa* and slid to a halt beside the ME's van. There were, in addition, two squad cars in front of the fortune-telling parlor, their rack lights hurling circus strobes of red, yellow and blue onto the snowy pavement, radios crackling and squawking to empty seats. The uniformed cops that had exited them were busily stringing crime scene tape between collapsible B.C.P.D. sawhorses, or standing by to provide backup for the detectives in command.

"You feel like taking this side of the street or the other?" Pembleton said, buttoning up and raising his collar against the wind. Vapor plumed from his mouth like a comic book word balloon.

"I *feel* like finding a diner and chugging down about ten hot cocoas in a row, never mind the whipped cream," Munch said.

Pembleton looked at him without expression.

"The other side of the street," Munch said, becoming less and less optimistic that he and Pembleton were going to make sweet music together. How he'd gotten talked into partnering up with the squad's resident gung-ho crusader, even temporarily, he'd never know.

Still without a word, Pembleton turned toward the hardware store next door to the *ofisa* and went inside, little entry bells tinkling over his head.

The owner was a skinny old guy with skin the color of strong coffee, tired, watery eyes and a gray stubble on his cheeks. Pembleton found him standing in the middle of a narrow aisle, dolefully shaking his head as he looked at a palmful of nails.

"You'd think folks'd know the difference by

now," he said without giving Pembleton an instant's glance.

"Excuse me, sir—"

"Name's Rollins. Ernest Rollins."

"Mr. Rollins," Pembleton said, waving his shield under his face, "I'm a detective checking on wheth—"

"It's 'bout near the turna' the century, ain't it?" said Rollins. "You got talkin' bank machines, kids playin' with them computers, *all* that fancy 'lectronic stuff, but people still ain't learned what's a nail and what's a screw, or at least they act that way when they come in here."

Suddenly craving another cigarette, Pembleton frowned with exasperation.

"Mr. Rollins—"

"Your screws, each an' every one of 'em, they got *grooves*, an' little notches up top on the head for the screw*driver*." Rollins said, plucking one out of a nearby bin with his free hand and holding it up to Pembleton as if he were a lecturer exhibiting a scientific specimen.

"Hell," he said, "you don't even have to have eyes to *see* it ain't no nail, long's you got fingers to *feel* it."

"Mr. Rollins—"

The shopkeeper continued in his pedantic mode, dropping the screw back where he'd gotten it, then taking a nail from the cluster in his open palm.

"Now, these things, they's smooth. Got no grooves, got no slots, got *nothin'* —"

"Mr. Rollins, please—"

Rollins sighed and dropped the nail into a separate bin from the screw—*clink!*

"Back when I started in this business," he went on, "your one-inch nails was called twopennies 'cause they sold *two* for a penny. By the same way a measurin', one-an'-a-quarter-inch nails was threepennies, one-an'-a-half-inch nails *fourpennies,* goin' on up to—"

"Mr. Rollins, I'm sorry to cut you off, but I'm sure you're aware that a man and woman were shot to death next door, and I'm trying to see whether you can help us with the case."

Rollins sighed and finally turned his moist eyes onto Pembleton.

"All I was gonna say, *if* youda let me, is that every time a customer tosses a screw in with the nails—or the other way round—insteada puttin' them back where they belong, it cost me money. Not much, maybe, 'cept with my rent goin' up to the moon, I can't afford t'lose a dime. This neighborhood, it *changin'.* I been here near fifty years, Detective, but blink your eyes and I'll be gone."

Pembleton met the shopkeeper's gaze and waited for him to finish.

"Gypsies moved in maybe a year, two years ago, an' do jus' fine sellin' their snake oil. Love, health, jobs, money, family problems—everybody worries 'bout them things. The fakes next door, they know it better'n I do. An' use what they know to hustle decent folks that *don't* know better."

Listening to the shopkeeper's bitter complaints, hearing the scorn in his voice, Pembleton felt somehow reduced. He wanted to grab the old man by the shoulders, make him see that his hatred would open a deep hole under his feet. But he was there to solve a murder, not spread kindness and brotherhood.

"Mr. Rollins, this is a double homicide," he said. "We're talking about a man and woman who, as far as we know, had no involvement at all with any fortune-telling operation."

"Maybe, maybe not," Rollins said. "An' maybe now they'll *all* pack up an' leave."

"Sir," Pembleton interrupted, "can you tell me what time you opened for business this morning?"

"Eight-thirty. Same's *every* morning."

"And when did you arrive at the shop?"

"'Bout a half hour before that."

Which was conveniently over *two* full hours after the murders occurred, Pembleton thought.

"Have you noticed any odd comings and goings next door recently?"

"No."

"Any visitors that stand out in your mind?"

"No."

"Had you heard your neighbors arguing at all?"

"No."

"Is there anything you feel might be important for me to know?"

"Yeah," the shopkeeper said. "I ain't a bit sorry 'bout what happened to them people."

Pembleton looked at him a moment, then suddenly decided to leave before the ground started to shake.

"Thank you," he said, then turned and went quickly out into the street.

THE TWO WOMEN in the travel agency next door offered Pembleton their own version of Rollins's see no evil, hear no evil, speak *plenty* of evil routine.

"They're nothing but cheap *parasites*," said the one who'd introduced herself as Mrs. Agostino. She was fiftyish, overweight and jowly and wore a puffed, sprayed coiffure that looked like a stale poundcake balanced on her head. "Let me tell you, Detective Pinkerton—"

"Pembleton," he corrected.

"Oh, sorry," she said. "Anyway, as I was saying, it's no wonder somebody'd want to put them in the cemetery."

"If they're *buried* in cemeteries," her younger colleague said. She was a tall, heavily made up woman named Mrs. Blair. "I mean, those people are strange."

Those people, Pembleton thought. Jesus, what else was new?

"Live in filth," Mrs. Agostino said. "None of them even have social security numbers."

"I thought you need a social security card to be legally declared dead," said Mrs. Blair. "Because

28

unless you're legally dead, I don't see how you can be buried."

"What does one have to do with the other?" said Mrs. Agostino.

"Dying and getting buried?" Mrs. Blair asked.

"No, no, having a social security card and being declared dead."

"It's for purposes of identification," said Mrs. Agostino. "The card, that is to say."

"Believe me, Ruthie, they have plenty of ID. Except it's all phoney."

"But what I'm telling you is . . ."

Pembleton stared at a poster of some exotic, palm-lined white-sand beach in Hawaii where a beautiful woman in a swimsuit was running exuberantly along the surf, her tanned skin covered with glistening beads of ocean spray, her hair fanning out in the breeze. A week of promising days and fulfilling nights at a package rate, airfare and hotel included, the ad copy read. Pembleton wondered if that wasn't exactly what he needed, if maybe he shouldn't call Mary and tell her to pack her suitcase, dress the baby and get ready for a vacation in paradise. He wondered if the cops in Hawaii had to deal with four hundred murders a year, and if the sprawling silvery-white beaches were ever stained with the blood of innocents.

". . . once had a friend whose husband became impotent, and some gypsy woman told her the problem could be cured with voodoo. . . ."

"You must be mistaken."

"About what?"

"Voodoo's what Haitians use. Or maybe people from New Orleans."

"All of sudden *you* know about *magic*?"

"No, I'm just explaining that—"

"Ladies," Pembleton broke in. Mrs. Blair's perfume was irritating his sinuses and he was anxious to get some fresh air. "Are you sure neither of you saw any strange visitors, or anything else that seemed unusual next door?"

"You mean this morning, Detective Pinkerton?"

"Pembleton."

"Excuse me?"

"My name's Pembleton. And I mean this morning, yesterday, last week or last month. *Whenever*."

The women shook their heads no.

"I'll leave you my card," he said wearily.

PEMBLETON'S LAST STOP on his side of the street was the corner bakery. He'd already been to four or five places besides the hardware store and travel agency, including a grocery, a dry cleaner and a copy center, every one of which yielded zilch in the way of leads.

D'Angelo's Italian Bakery had windows on two sides jammed with cookies, cannolis, tarts, fruitcakes, and a dozen loaves of bread. Though Pembleton had thought his appetite had been robbed by the futility of his morning's efforts, it declared itself present and accounted for the moment he got a look at the assortment of creamy desserts exhibited before him.

He pushed through the door, was greeted by a medley of delectable baking smells that made his stomach jump and paw like a dog begging at the dinner table, and wondered if his wife would like some pastries with her coffee that night.

"May I help you?"

Pembleton tore his eyes from a tray of Napoleons in the glass counter and flashed his tin at the kid standing near the register. He was maybe nineteen or twenty and very fit looking, with tousled black hair, handsome features and sky-blue eyes that probably scored him as many dates as his toned physique.

"I'm investigating the murders down the block," Pembleton said.

"Wow, no kidding," the kid said, leaning forward to study the badge. "You with Homicide?"

"I am."

"Wow," the kid repeated.

"May I ask your name, son?"

"Tony," he said. "Last name's D'Angelo, like on the awning outside. My family runs this place." He paused. "Well, nowadays it's pretty much me and my mother."

"Tony, I only have a few questions." Pembleton pocketed the leather case containing his badge and got out his pad. "What time did you get you here this morning?"

"Maybe five o'clock, five-thirty."

"That early?" Pembleton looked at him hopefully. He was the first person he'd quizzed thus far who had been in the area at the approximate time of the killings—or who'd *admitted* to having been in the area, anyway.

"Sure." The kid shrugged. "The baking takes a while. All our stuff's made fresh every day, and whatever we don't sell goes to Saint Ignatius. That's a church a few blocks away runs a homeless shelter."

"Are you a member of the parish?"

"Uh-uh," D'Angelo said. "Mom and I live out near the bay. But the priest at Saint Ignatius, he started up this drive, got a bunch of local businesses to give donations."

Pembleton nodded and scratched a note into his pad.

"By the way, how do you get to work? Do you hop a bus, use the subway—"

"I drive. Usually park around the corner."

"And your mother? Does she drive in with you?"

"Once, twice a week," the kid said. "My father died about six months ago and it took a lot out of her. So she usually comes in a little later."

"And today?"

"Today I drove in alone. Mom won't be here for—" He looked at his wrist, frowned.

"Anything wrong?"

"Must've forgotten my watch," he said. "Anyway, she ought to be here in an hour or so."

Pembleton jotted away with his pencil. *Scritch-scratch.*

"Getting back to this morning," he said, "did you notice anything out of the ordinary when you arrived?"

The kid thought a moment, shook his head.

"Was there anybody besides yourself on the street?" Pembleton asked.

"You mean, like, a stranger?"

"Or someone you're acquainted with. Another shop owner, a delivery truck driver—it doesn't matter."

The kid started to shake his head again, then hesitated.

"Well . . . ," he said, his brow furrowing.

Pembleton waited.

"I was just thinking," D'Angelo said. "I *did* see somebody a little while after I got here. The daughter. But I didn't figure—"

"*Whose* daughter?" Pembleton looked at him steadily.

"The Gypsy that lives upstairs from the place. Heavy guy with dark hair."

"Mihial Bash?"

The kid shrugged. "I guess. Couldn't really tell you their names."

"By his daughter, do you mean a pretty girl, long black hair, maybe a few years older than yourself?"

"That sure sounds like her. Got a figure that won't quit. She's different from the rest of them, you know what I mean. Doesn't come around here much."

"And you saw her *when*?"

33

"Quarter to six, six o'clock."

Which was three hours before she claimed to have driven in from Washington, Pembleton thought.

Scritch-scratch.

"Are you absolutely *sure* about this?"

"Positive. I usually let myself in through the back door, turn the lights on in the pastry kitchen, then come out here and take care of a few things. That's when I saw her drive past in the Mustang."

"Mustang?"

"Yeah. A beaut. Nineteen sixty-three, maybe sixty-four, convertible, electric blue, cherry condition. That's why I remember seeing her this morning. . . . I always notice the wheels."

"Did she park? Get out of the car?"

"Uh-uh. Matter of fact, she seemed to be taking off in a hurry." D'Angelo gestured vaguely toward the front window. "Heading toward Thatcher Street."

"Was she alone, or was someone in the car with her?"

"Well, she was definitely *driving.*" D'Angelo scratched behind his ear. "There might've been a person in the passenger seat, but I couldn't tell you for sure. It was still dark out. And she went by pretty fast."

Pembleton's eyebrows arched. He felt a cold draft of air behind him as the door swung open and a customer walked in.

"What else do you remember?" he said.

"That's about it. I get busy, you know."

"And you didn't hear any sounds that might have been gunshots this morning?"

"No." The kid looked past him at the woman who'd entered and gave her a familiar wave. "Nothing like that at all."

"Okay, thanks." Pembleton finished writing his notes and slid the pad back into his coat pocket. "If I need more of a statement, I'll be back."

D'Angelo nodded, and was turning toward his customer when Pembleton suddenly remembered that he'd wanted to bring something home for his wife.

"Wait," he said.

The kid did an about-face.

"Do you have anything with a pineapple filling?" Pembleton asked.

PEMBLETON WAS STEPPING back outside, bakery box in hand, when he noticed Munch leaving a store across the street and called to him. He was through working his side of the block and figured he'd help with the rest of the interviews.

As it turned out, Munch had nearly wrapped things up himself and was heading toward his final stop, a stationery store diagonally opposite D'Angelo's.

They went in together.

The place was owned and run by a Hasidic couple in their thirties named Putnitsky—the husband a bearded man wearing a black suit, white shirt and yarmulke, Mrs. Putnitsky a diminutive woman with mousy brown hair.

"*Rehdn deer Yiddish?*" Mr. Putnisky asked Munch.

"*Ah beesel.*"

Putnitsky smiled. "A Jewish Homicide cop, eh? What's next, an Irish rabbi?"

Hardy-har-har, Munch thought, annoyed that the guy had pegged him as a landsman, since he preferred to think of himself as Waspishly good-looking in a Robert Redford vein.

He went down the standard list of questions with them—were you, did you, do you, where, when, what—but at first neither seemed able to provide a shred of relevent information. They'd gotten to work after the crime occurred, noticed nothing unusual, had virtually no contact with the people that ran the fortune-telling parlor and could only express sadness that the murdered Gypsies had left behind a daughter who would now be orphaned. . . .

"Hold on a sec," Munch said. "*What* daughter?"

"Their *only* one," Mr. Putnitsky said. "At least I think she's an only child."

"Such a cute little girl too," Mrs. Putnitsky added with a tsking sound. "*Gotinyu,* I can't imagine how terrible it would be having your parents shot to death."

Munch and Pembleton traded puzzled glances.

"Are both of you sure you're thinking of the right people?" Pembleton asked.

"Absolutely," Mr. Putnitsky said. "They were building superintendents over on Belvedere Place."

"Positively," his wife agreed. "I saw the husband all the time, sweeping, cleaning, bagging the trash for the sanitation trucks."

"He *seemed* hardworking."

"Which, let me tell you, is exceptional for those people."

Pembleton could scarcely believe how often he'd heard the phrase *those people* repeated over the past few hours, especially since it had, for the most part, been coming from ethnic types who'd been called the very same thing, probably in the same disparaging manner, by one persecutor or another throughout history. He also found it startling that not *one* of the victims' relatives had said a word about their having left behind a daughter . . . and wondered what the reason for the familial secrecy might be, assuming the Putnitskys weren't, in fact, mistaken about the child's existence.

"How old is this girl?" he asked.

"Fourteen, fifteen," said Mrs. Putnitsky. "Something like that."

Both detectives were silent awhile. Behind the counter, Mr. Putnitsky slit open a carton with a box opener and began unpacking bottles of Liquid Paper.

Munch stood there quietly a moment longer, then said, "Mr. and Mrs. Putnitsky, it's important that you be particularly certain about what you're telling us."

"They had a daughter," Mrs. Putnitsky declared

emphatically. "You can take our word for it, Detective."

Munch and Pembleton looked at each other.

"We got some work to do," Pembleton said.

"Oy," Munch said.

"SO," MUNCH SAID, "you never told me whether you believe in curses."

They were driving back to the station, Munch behind the wheel, Pembleton riding shotgun with the pastry box on his lap, the tires of their unmarked car sloshing through snow that was already turning the color of exhaust smoke.

"Not that crap again," Pembleton said. He was looking straight ahead out the windshield.

"Hey, it's a simple question."

"Do I believe in curses?"

"Uh-huh. Gypsy spells. Hexes. Evil eyes."

"Kind that can bring you bad luck? Ruin your life?"

"Uh-huh."

"Or turn you into a werewolf?"

"In extreme cases." Munch said, slowing as he approached a red light.

Pembleton rubbed his chin.

"Tell you what I think," he said. "I think every person in this world's got a dog nobody else can see."

Munch shot him a glance. "A *what*?"

"A dog," Pembleton said. "At least it looks like a dog. . . . I won't dignify this beast by calling it a

38

wolf. It's a mean, stupid, surly, scruffy mutt with bloodshot eyes, an ear that got chewed up in a fight, maybe some flies buzzing around its head."

"Oh," Munch said, thinking that he'd asked for it. "And it's invisible?"

"That's right. An invisible dog on an invisible leash."

"Oh."

"Sometimes it pulls one way, sometimes another," Pembleton said. "Pulls till your arm feels like it's gonna come right out of its socket."

A plow truck clanked across the intersection, its shovel scraping the blacktop. Munch drummed his fingers on the wheel, impatient for the light to change.

"Here's this guy walking along, trying to mind his business, when his dog sniffs some food and jerks him in that direction, forget that it's in another dog's bowl," Pembleton said. "Another guy's mutt sees a female dog that wants no part of its ugly, flea-bitten kisser, but it howls and tugs at the leash until this guy gives in, lets it run him right into busy traffic, lets it pounce her."

Munch looked at him across the front seat.

"These dogs, no matter how well you treat them, they always want what isn't being offered, or belongs to somebody else," Pembleton said. "And to get what they want, they bully, they fight, they steal, they kill. It's their nature. Consequences don't matter, because they aren't afraid of punishment.

God made them greedy, impulsive things. All they know are claws and teeth."

"Think I'll take mine to the pound," Munch said.

Pembleton shook his head. "Doesn't work that way. Each of us is stuck with his own."

"Great," Munch said, wondering if Pembleton had cut back too drastically on his nicotine intake. "So what do we do with the little monsters?"

"Well, there are only two choices." Pembleton was still looking out the window. "You can let it drag you wherever the hell it wants, or you can plant your feet on the ground and pull in the leash. Yank that nasty mongrel back with all your strength. Make it *heel*, no matter how long or hard it fights you." He sighed. "Light's green, by the way."

Munch realized he'd twisted around in his seat and was staring at Pembleton. He settled back, returned his eyes to the road and slid the car forward through the surging traffic.

"Serious shit," he said contemplatively.

"Uh-huh."

"You make that up just now?"

Pembleton grinned.

"Uh-huh," he said.

FOUR

EXCEPT FOR THE Board, a snapshot of the Baltimore
Homicide Unit's squad room would have shown it
to be virtually indistinguishable from any other big
city police HQ: institutional green walls; practical
gray steel desks, file cabinets and lockers; func-
tional glass office partitions hung with slatted
blinds that could be drawn for a modicum of
privacy. The checkerboard linoleum floor had been
scuffed and scarred by the pacing of innumerable
feet. There was a standing coat rack near the entry,
a water cooler in one corner, a coffeemaker in
another; a long wall lined with contoured plastic
chairs cramming witnesses beside suspects, and
suspects beside the sobbing friends and relatives of
those they were believed to have murdered. There
were other universals of police work that even the
clearest of photos would entirely fail to impart, such
as the ceaselessly ringing phones and clattering
typewriters, the decades-old smell of nervous sweat

41

and cigarette smoke that clung to every wall and fixture, the grim, grinding routines of men and women whose lives were spent sorting through the messes left when human beings turned other human beings into dead bodies.

The Board, however, was unique, looming over the BHU murder cops on Lt. Al Giardello's shift like the first set of holy tablets given to Moses on Mount Sinai, testimony to their innate worthiness, constant reminder of the path of grace, yet ready to come down on their heads if they stinted in their duties and were seduced by the demons of laziness and indifference. In fact, it would not be overly stretching the metaphor to state that, like the biblical covenant, the Board's fundamental, overarching purpose was to keep the murder cops honest.

A rectangular white marker board with a glossy Melamine surface, it dominated an entire wall of the squad room and had Giardello's name printed across the top above a horizontal ruled line, below which were several vertical columns, each one headed by the name of a detective on his shift, of whom there were presently seven: Russert, Kellerman, Howard, Lewis, Munch, Pembleton and Bayliss. Pick a detective at random, and he (or she) would typically have anywhere from one to a dozen names below his (or her) own, some written in erasable red marker ink, others in more permanent black ink. These listings were the key elements of this chart, the names of the slain citizens of Baltimore whose murders had fallen upon the cops to handle. Closed cases written in black, open cases in red, each matched to the primary investigator as on an accounting ledger. . . . Although to Frank Pembleton the choice of colors had a deeper, subtler and perhaps more poignant significance.

To Pembleton the red was that of envy, lust, rage, passion and the blood that was too often spilled when those powerful human emotions were let out of the cage.

To Pembleton the black represented finality, closure and perhaps the blessing of eternal rest for the souls of those whose killers had been brought to justice.

Though his reputation as a supercop stemmed primarily from a string of successes that had put him well in the black for years, it was the names written in red that leaped out at Pembleton when he reported to the station every day, the names written in red that blazed before his eyes as if scrawled in apocalyptic flame, the names written in red that burned their way into his mind so that they shimmered before him even when his eyelids were closed, searing through the blackness of his long and restless nights.

He'd been back from the scene of the Bash murders less than fifteen minutes, and had barely finished making his entry of the victims in bright red ink, when he blew up at Munch in front of everyone in the room. What pushed him to it was something he accidentally overheard Munch asking Bayliss, who looked zombified coming off his temporary shift and was getting ready to go home and hit the sack.

Setting aside the issue of whether it really warranted the level of anger it provoked, the question was classic Munch:

"Hey, Timmy-boy," he'd said, "you know any good local restaurants that serve Gypsy cuisine?"

Bayliss had paused on his way to the door and looked at him.

"Huh?" he said blearily.

"Gypsy cuisine. Classic or nouveau, doesn't make a difference to me."

Bayliss blinked as if he'd been awakened from sleepwalking.

"What's Gypsy cuisine?" he asked. With his brush-cut hair and boyish features he looked like a grown up Mousketeer, all scrubbed innocence, only his haunted eyes betraying the corrosive toll of working the murder beat and being too often reminded of the dark side of human nature. A year or so back he'd grown a beard to toughen his good guy image, but it had felt as if he were wearing a cheap paste-on disguise, and he'd since shaved it off.

"Gypsy *food*," Munch said from behind his desk.

Bayliss frowned at him.

"Thanks so much for clarifying," he said. "What I meant—like you didn't know, Professor—was *what sort* of cooking is that? As a matter of curiosity. Is it spicy, saucy, vegetarian—"

"I have no idea."

"No idea?"

"None," Munch said. "Which brings me back to my question—"

"Why don't you just check the phone book?" Bayliss asked, yawning.

"Have it right here, matter of fact."

Munch rotated in his swivel chair, bent over a copy of the yellow pages on his blotter and started running his finger down the page to which it was opened.

"Looking under G," he said, "there's German, and there's Greek, but then it jumps right to Health food, Hungarian, Italian—"

"Has it occurred to you that maybe there's no *demand* for Gypsy food?"

"No demand," Munch repeated, looking at Bayliss as if he'd just voiced his belief in the flat earth theory. "In all of Charm City?"

"Uh-uh," Bayliss said. "Not anywhere."

"That doesn't make sense." Munch jabbed his finger at the yellow pages. "I mean, you'd think that if there are enough people wanting to eat at a Senegalese place, which I see listed right here, then you'd have enough for a Gyp—"

"Where's Senegal, anyway?" Bayliss yawned again.

"I dunno," Munch said. "Never heard of it. Which is exactly what I was getting at—"

"It's in West Africa," Megan Russert said, coming over to Munch's desk from the coffee machine. Quick, smart and in her mid-thirties, with cool

45

blond hair and notoriously good legs, she looked sexy just standing there blowing on her steaming hot cup.

Munch looked at her. He liked Russert, who'd been promoted and demoted so often he'd lost track of her rank, which he believed was currently a notch or two below his own, but might, for all he knew, also be *above* his this morning, which was why he always hedged his bet and tried to avoid offending her. On the other hand, he *hated* when she showed off her highfalutin educational and professional credentials, which included graduating third in her class from the Naval Academy and subsequently landing a job in Intelligence. Not to mention, of course, the silver citation she'd received for busting a citywide ring of massage parlors when working in Narcotics.

"That so?" he asked, wishing she hadn't butted in just as he was about to make his point.

"A *country* in West Africa, way on the coast," she elaborated. "The capital's Dakar."

"Hey, thanks. But that's really got nothing to do with what I was asking, which is whether Bayliss here knows about any Gypsy restaurants——"

"Why'd you ask *me*?" Bayliss yawned again.

"Because you've dated a lot of women," Munch said. "Ipso facto, you eat out a lot."

"Oh," Bayliss said receptively. "Actually, I can recommend this great Cajun joint——"

"That's really nice, Tim, but she's a Gypsy."

"*Who's* a Gypsy?"

"The woman I'm taking to dinner this weekend."

That was when Pembleton finally reached the end of his fuse.

"What the hell is that supposed to mean, Munch?" he said, *snarled* actually, turning from the Board with the red marker still in his hand.

"Huh?" Munch said.

"What's *dating* a woman who's a Gypsy got to do with taking her out to eat Gypsy *food*?"

Munch spread his hands.

"Well," he said, "I figured—"

"If you have a date with a black woman . . . or for that matter, if you go out to eat somewhere with *me* . . . does that mean the place has to serve ham hocks and black-eyed peas, maybe some fried chicken wings for an appetizer?"

"Frank—"

"Maybe if I'm asking *you* out to lunch I better make sure there's matzo balls and lox on the menu."

"Frank—"

"Or being as Kay happens to be of *Irish* descent, I suppose you think she only eats cabbage and potatoes," Pembleton continued, gesturing toward Detective Kay Howard, who obliviously looked up from the file she'd been studying at her desk, her thick red hair sweeping back in a cloud.

"Frank, relax," Munch said, convinced Pembleton was going through severe nicotine withdrawal. "I was only—"

"I'll bet Lieutenant Giardello would be a real dilemma for you." Pembleton had propped his hands on Munch's desk and was practically yelling in his face. "A black Italian, what the hell is *he* gonna eat? Chitlins in *marinara* sauce? Or maybe—"

"Frank, man, what's the problem?" Bayliss said in a calm voice, putting a hand on his shoulder.

Pembleton took a deep breath and looked at him squarely.

"Ignorance," he said.

"Look," Munch said, "just because I didn't know where to find a Gypsy restaurant—"

Pembleton rolled his eyes.

"I think Frank was talking about your preconceptions," Bayliss said to Munch.

"*What* preconceptions?"

"The ones that make you assume a Gypsy would only want to go out for Gypsy food," Bayliss said quietly. "Whatever that may be."

Munch sat there a moment, an expression of dawning comprehension on his face.

"Oh," he said finally. "I get it."

"In Munch's defense," Megan said, swallowing some coffee, "he never said she'd *only* want—"

"The issue of ethnic stereotypes aside," Frank said to Munch, "I don't like the idea of you dating a possible suspect in an ongoing investigation."

"Hold on a minute." Munch sat up straight in his chair. "Since when is Lovera Bash a suspect?"

"I said *possible* suspect," Pembleton corrected.

"And I said *since when*?"

"Since she withheld information about the victims in this case having a daughter."

Munch shook his head, "Now, that's where you're wrong, Frank. We never asked her about any kid."

"We spoke to three members of the Bash family, right?"

Munch nodded.

"Doesn't it seem reasonable to think somebody ought to have mentioned the girl?" Frank said.

"Well, that's a whole different issue," Munch said. "Why should Vera Bash have been the one?"

"I'm not saying Vera *necessarily*," Frank said. "I'm saying *somebody*."

Munch sighed. "Granted, Frank, it's a little weird. But that doesn't mean any of them were involved in the murder . . . Vera, least of all."

"Why? Why is she less suspicious than her father, for instance?"

"Because she isn't the type. She's a college professor, for chrissake."

"So was the Unabomber, according to the FBI," Frank said.

Munch looked at him.

"Touché," Russert said, and walked off toward her desk.

"Also, I have reason to believe Vera Bash may have lied to us about something else."

"*Actually* lied?"

Pembleton nodded and summarized what Tony D'Angelo had said about having seen her drive by his shop, over three hours before she claimed to have arrived in Baltimore.

"D'Angelo also thought he saw another person in the car with her," he concluded.

Munch raised his eyebrows.

"The girl?"

"That," Pembleton said, "is for us to find out."

Munch sighed and flipped shut his phone book.

"Guess Miss Bash and I won't be falling short of dinner conversation," he said.

"I guess not," Frank said with a small smile.

Bayliss yawned a third time, stretching his arms out wide.

"Glad to see you boys are playing nice again," he said groggily, and then turned and walked out the door before either of them could reply.

FIVE

"I DUG UP the name of the department's Gypsy specialist," Lt. Al Giardello said, exiting the cubicle that passed for his office and coming over to Pembleton's desk.

Pembleton looked up from the typewriter on which he was pecking out his case report. He'd been concentrating on getting the facts of the Bash murders down, and the sudden appearance of Giardello—or 'G,' as his crew called him for short—had startled him. Nothing new there; between the sneakers he always wore despite his tough insistence on a dress code, and his deep, tubalike voice, the loot had a way of quietly stealing up on you, then announcing himself with a bellow that unfailingly gave the squad room's regulars a jolt, and made visitors and newcomers jump off their bones.

"Didn't know we had a Gypsy specialist," Pembleton said.

He typed the end of a sentence with one finger and read it back to himself with a grunt of satisfaction.

"His name's Harry Grogan, works out of Western," Giardello said, and handed Pembleton a slip of paper torn from his memo pad. "Give him a call."

"Sure." Pembleton had already shuffled aside the memo with Grogan's phone number on it, and resumed looking over his report.

Giardello frowned, then reached across the desk and slid the phone number back in front of Pembleton.

"Maybe I ought to expand on what I said."

Pembleton glanced up at him again. Giardello was amping up for a basso roar that he feared would cause the building's foundations to tremble apart at a submolecular level.

"No need," Pembleton lifted the memo sheet off his blotter. "I'll get in touch with him right now."

Giardello grinned triumphantly and padded back to his office on sneakered feet.

A moment or two later Pembleton got up, went over to where Munch was sitting and slapped the little square of paper onto his desk.

"Who's Harry Grogan?" Munch said, studying G's aggressive penmanship.

"Gypsy expert, Western District," Pembleton said. "Give him a buzz, pronto."

"What am I supposed to say when I get hold of him?"

Pembleton shrugged. "Tell him we'd like to consult."

Munch sighed, lifted the receiver off his phone and punched Grogan's number into the console.

"Yeah?" someone answered on the third ring.

"Harry Grogan, please."

"That'd be me." Grogan's gruff, phlegmy voice sounded like a drain clogged with bacon grease. "Who's this?"

"Detective John Munch, Southern District Homicide. We've got a double murder involving Gypsies on our hands."

"They the perps or the vics?"

"Victims. Well, maybe the perps too, I don't know. We've just started the investigation."

Munch explained about Mihial Bash's blaming a rival clan called the Demetros for the slayings.

"Isn't too far-fetched," Grogan said. "Rival *kumpanias* can be touchy with each other."

"*Kum*-what?"

"*Kumpanias*. Extended families that live and work together. No telling how far a dispute could go once it builds up steam."

"Oh." Munch considered that a second. "Are we talking *crime* families, like the mob?"

"Yes and no, it gets complicated," Grogan said. "I think we oughtta talk about this face-to-face. Before this thing turns into an all-out war."

"War?" Munch knew he sounded like a parrot, but these were fortune-tellers they were talking about, not gangbangers, and he had yet to hear of Gypsy women in headscarfs shooting up each other's storefronts with Uzis. "Are you serious?"

"Like I said, we should get together. You free tonight?"

"Well, I suppose. I go off duty after five."

"Me too. Let's make it for six. There's this bar I like, the Shamrock, and it's at—"

"Actually," Munch said. "I run my own saloon, so why don't we meet there?"

"I thought you said you were a Homicide bull?"

"I did," Munch said. "And I am."

"Cream of the crop, Charm City's elite," Grogan said.

Munch was silent.

"And you're a *bar* owner?"

"I don't see the contradiction," Munch said.

"Seems frivolous to me, is all."

"Well, what can I say?"

"That you'll meet me at the Shamrock, for one thing."

Munch wasn't sure whether he was more irritated or offended. "What's wrong with my place?"

"I don't know your place. What's it called, anyway?"

"The Waterfront."

"Like I said, never heard of it."

Munch sighed. "You can take my word—"

"It's just that I can't be sure I'll like the atmosphere."

"We've got atmosphere up the kazoo," Munch said. "In fact, the building's a certified landmark."

"Oh yeah?" Grogan sounded skeptical. "How so?"

"George Washington took a leak there once," Munch said proudly. "You can check with the Historical Society if you don't believe me."

The line was silent a moment.

"Let me tell you something," Grogan said finally, a discernible edge in his voice. "If Washington pissing someplace once makes it a landmark, then the Shamrock's gotta be considered a fucking national *monument*, 'cause I've taken a good shit there plenty of times. Now, you wanna get the skinny on Gypsies—and lemme tell you, you better for your own good—we'll meet where I say. All right?"

Munch quashed an urge to give the jerk the raspberries through the receiver.

"Yeah," he said, taking a deep breath. "Sure."

"Great," Grogan said. "Here's the address. . . ."

HE HADN'T MEANT to kill them, hadn't meant to kill anyone, that had been just plain bad luck. Not that they hadn't deserved it after what they'd done. There were times when you had no choice, times when all your choices were taken away, and you had to take things in hand without worrying about the consequences, either that or get squashed like a cockroach. That was the position they'd put him in.

Still, he'd never figured it would come to shooting those two. They weren't supposed to be there, *nobody* was; he'd wanted to get in, take what he'd come for, and get out. The gun had only been for protection. He'd planned it through, watched the street to make sure he wouldn't bump into any of them, waited until he'd seen the old man leave . . . but it had been so dark, there'd been so much snow, they could have been coming up the block even while he was working open the door. And when they surprised him, walking in out of the snow, the guy, the *husband*, the way he'd charged, it was like he thought bullets couldn't drill through his skin, and then after he started fighting like a maniac, hitting, and they'd been rolling around on the floor, and especially when the husband had smacked him in the face, everything had turned red and all the hate had swelled up in him and he'd lost control and popped the son of a bitch. . . .

And why should he feel guilty about Christine? She'd been screaming at the top of her lungs, and would have screamed until someone heard, until the goddamned law came running. Then afterward, if he'd just taken off and let her be, she'd have been able to identify him. Why should he feel guilty?

Yeah, it was their fault, not his. *Theirs.* And it still wasn't over for him, not as long as there might be evidence, evidence he'd left behind. He was scared all the time now, scared deep down inside himself, and when he looked in the mirror it was like seeing a stranger, somebody he didn't even know. It was a curse, a terrible fucking curse, and he'd either have to shake it or go crazy. Otherwise he'd be walking around deathly afraid for the next fifty years, the rest of his fucking life maybe, always looking over his shoulder, breaking into a cold sweat every time he saw his own shadow.

Somehow, he had to get rid of the fear and the guilt.

It hadn't been his fault.

In the end, everybody had to worry about their own.

"THE THING TO remember about Gypsies is they don't want in," Grogan was explaining to Munch. "Generally speaking, of course."

He stuffed some food into his mouth and, hardly chewing, sloshed it down with a gulp of beer.

Munch sat across from Grogan and stared into his own plate, trying to avoid watching Grogan eat and thereby preserve what little appetite he had. With his grimy clothes, gurgly voice and huge slopping gut, Grogan reminded him of a bathtub filled with dirty water.

In many respects, so did the Shamrock. The place was a seedy watering-hole in a Reservoir Hill neighborhood that had washed up stranded between ghettoization and gentrification as the city's slipping economy brought development to a halt. The seams of its uneasy social fabric were visible and strained; on the streets outside, working-class African-

Americans, Lithuanians and Irishmen would exchange disdainful stares, with all three groups looking suspiciously upon the sprinkling of white-collar types that had arrived during the boom years of the eighties.

Inside the bar, however, time might have come to a standstill twenty years before. The ethnic mix was Irish, Irish and more Irish. On the mirror behind the horseshoe bar were plastic shamrocks, pro-IRA stickers, an ancient and yellowed Paul McCartney poster, and about the only thing Munch figured for a recent addition, a laminated 8X10 glossy of some English-looking castle going up in flames. Running the length of the room were dim, flyspecked light fixtures, torn leatherette stools with their guts bleeding out and empty beer kegs that had been stacked against the walls for so long they were on the verge of becoming petrified. The floor was covered with mountains of sawdust and there were some booths in back near the pool table.

Grogan had been sitting at one of those booths when Munch arrived and had immediately waved him over, probably tagging him as the Homicide cop he'd spoken with on the phone because he was the only guy in the dump—including Grogan himself—who didn't look as if he thought flannel shirts and mackinaws were the height of fashion, and a romantic night out with the wife was treating her to the Sizzler all-you-can-eat special.

"Gypsies want to keep their boundaries with

non-Gypsies solid," Grogan continued now that his food had been washed down his gullet. "If they cross 'em, it's only for what you'd call economic reasons. See, according to tradition, they can't make money off each other. Which leaves everybody else as fair game for their cons."

He paused and looked at Munch, a grin on his shiny red face, obviously enjoying the chance to hold forth.

"You should eat some of your food," he said. "It's damn tasty."

Munch willed his hand toward his fork. The dish in front of him—the *only* dish to be served out of the Shamrock's four-star kitchen tonight—was meatballs and gravy on egg noodles, a bizarre combination that not even his mother, whom he'd always believed had cooked as an act of pure sadism, had ever conceived of.

Grogan watched him eat with cheerful satisfaction.

"Those bastards been scamming outsiders for five hundred years," he said. "Even the *word* Gypsy is rooted in bullshit, you know."

"How's that?" Munch chewed mechanically.

"Comes from *Egyptians*."

"Isn't Egypt where they originated? Their ancestors, I mean."

"That's what most people think, and, like I was starting to say, it's also their first big lie," Grogan said. "Far as anybody knows, Gypsies started out as a northern Indian tribe. Maybe a thousand years ago they took the losing side in a fracas between a local king and some Muslim out-of-towners, and had to book to save their hides. Been traveling light ever since."

He finished his beer and signaled for the bartender, who was watching the inaudible television set above the counter while polishing a glass with a rag Munch suspected he also used for scrubbing the toilet.

"By the time they reach Europe around the fifteenth century, they're selling themselves as Christian refugees driven outta Nile country by a Muslim jihad, keeping just enough truth in their story to make it wash with the Holy Roman Emperor," Grogan said. "Can't say I blame 'em, because otherwise nobody'd have let the poor slobs past the border."

"But people soon came to love and welcome them without prejudice, and everyone lived together happily ever after."

"Funny guy," Grogan said.

"You mean they didn't?" Munch said with mock surprise.

"Actually, it wasn't so bad for Gypsies at first. They were tradesmen, mainly blacksmiths and musicians, and a lot of nobles gave them work around the court." Grogan speared a noodle with his fork and shrugged. "Course, pretty soon the local authorities change. Plus Gypsies are havin' kids, an' their kids are havin' more kids, and somebody notices one too many dark faces in the neighborhood, and starts bitchin' that the darkies are taking away jobs—"

"Same old same old," Munch said.

Grogan nodded. "Next thing you know, Gypsies are banned from employment, what you'd call undesirables, with no way of existin' within the system. So they go *outside* it. Since they already got this image of havin' some kinda connection to the supernatural, they use it on the rubes, offer to hire out their so-called magic powers for cash."

"Wisdom of the savage," Munch said.

"Somethin' like that."

Munch sat there quietly for a few seconds. An arm brushed against him and a guy with breath like scotch and ashes slurred an apology into his face. At the bar an old souse with eyes like runny eggs was flapping his withered, liver-spotted fist at an invisible opponent. Some coins were deposited into the pool table and the balls tumbled from inside it with a loud *chunk*.

Finally the bartender arrived with the fresh round Grogan had ordered, dropped a pair of cardboard coasters onto the table between the two cops, set their beers on the coasters and rapped the table with his knuckles.

"These're on me, Harry," he said, and turned back to the bar without waiting for a thank-you.

Grogan took a long draft and wiped his mouth with his palm.

"Ahhh," he said, his smile all teeth. "Now, what was I tellin' you?"

"About the Gypsies creating an alternative economy."

"Yeah, right."

"In a way, it's the same thing the Jews did," Munch reflected aloud.

"Except they were always lookin' to join the mainstream, and came up with ways of makin' a living that would put 'em there, or at least close to it. The Gypsies never gave up bein' nomads. It's just a cultural difference. Like I told you before, they don't want in." He regarded Munch seriously. "I'll tell 'you somethin' though. They been shit on as much as any group in history, maybe more so. Three hundred years ago the fucking Slovaks executed all their women and locked their children away in so-called hospitals. Nobody knows how many thousands of 'em Hitler threw into the ovens. Back in the eighties, in Hungary, I think, hard-core skinheads went sackin' and burnin' in Gypsy ghettos without a peep outta the government. Same thing in Romania a few years back, when that scumbag Iliescu incited the public against 'em, let 'em take the heat for his corruption. . . ."

"Let's cut to last night, right here in Baltimore," Munch said. "There are two dead people who happen to be Gypsies, and according to at least one member of their family, it wasn't outsiders that killed them, but other Gypsies."

"Yeah, I already got that from you," Grogan said, displeased with having been interrupted. "What's the question?"

"The question's *why*," Munch said. "Why would two clans be going at it?"

"That's easy," Grogan said. "Turf. They're territorial, like guppies, gangbangers, pigeons, politicians, an' all God's other fine creatures."

Munch nodded and drank some beer.

"Gypsy clans are into all kinds of organized rackets," Grogan went on. "Fortune-tellin' swindles are the most well known, but there's also real-estate scams, welfare fraud, counterfeiting . . . even out-and-out theft, blackmail and murder."

"Can you give me any examples?" Munch said.

"How much time you got?" Grogan said. "Here's a doozy from the bag of tricks—last year a group of 'em got nailed for runnin' a high-tech black widow operation. Their point woman was this really hot-lookin' broad, maybe twenty-five or -six. She'd hook up with rich old widowers on the Internet, marry 'em, poison 'em, and make off with the inheritance. Split the millions with her relatives, who did the online research."

"How generous of her," Munch said, and speared a meatball with his fork.

"Back to the subject of competition, the rule in most cities is that no two kin groups can have their parlors closer'n three blocks from each other. Once in a while you get a powerful *kumpania* runs the

63

whole town. Like when King Tene Bimbo's bunch had a lock on Chicago."

"Tene *Bimbo*? That a real name?"

"Real as the bristles on my balls," Grogan said.

Munch halted his fork's trajectory halfway to his mouth and let it sink back down to his plate, the image conjured by Grogan's remark killing what little appetite he'd worked up.

"Whatsamatter?" Grogan asked.

"Nothing," Munch said. "Tell me about King Tene."

"He was the meanest, toughest, crookedest son-ovabitch in the Midwest during the twenties and thirties. Even Capone was afraid to fuck with him. Tene bulled his way to the top rung of a dozen tribes, took a percentage of every Gypsy operation in the Midwest as tribute. Anybody dumb enough to get in his way wound up in the hospital, and that's if he was lucky. While most folks were resoling their shoes with cardboard on account of the Depression, Tene was bein' chauffeured around in a fleet of Caddies and Lincolns." Grogan sighed almost admiringly. "In the 1950s things finally got too hot for King Tene in Chicago and he shuffled off to New York, got his criminal activities rolling there. Lived to a ripe old age too. When his ticker finally quit on him in '69, his funeral procession held up traffic with an eight-man band playin' 'The Battle Hymn of the Republic,' an' a police escort authorized by the mayor."

"The king of kings have a princely heir?" Munch asked.

"His son was some kinda lowlife twit who didn't amount to squat." Grogan's face screwed up with disgust. "I tell you, the genes of great men are always watered down in their kids. Lookit Kirk and Michael Douglas, f'rinstance. Dad's a fucking giant. Gives us *Spartacus, Town Without Pity* and *Lust for Life*. But what do we get from his son? Garbage like *Romancing the Stone* and—"

"Who's boss nowadays?"

"Nobody," Grogan said. "About fifteen years ago a slick Oregon *baro*—that's a local Gypsy leader— passed himself off for a while as 'King of the Western North American Gypsies,' even got invited to Reagan's inauguration. But that was jive." Grogan laughed. "P.S., he finagled a bunch of minority grants outta the feds, all of which went to line his pockets."

"So if the new kid on the block decides to open a fortune-telling parlor where somebody else already has a stake, there's no authority figure to settle the problem?"

"Like I said, you got *baros* for that. Guys who are respected by all the feudin' parties. The *baro* will usually call a tribal council, try to iron things out." Grogan picked up his beer, saw that it was empty and frowned. "Sometimes the beef gets settled, sometimes it don't. Depends on the offense, and how high the thermostat's been turned up on everyone's temper. Which, by the way, makes me wonder about your little problem."

Munch waited.

"When Gypsies get into a heavy row with each other, they don't make distinctions between what's business and what's personal. If it comes down to violence, they like it up close. Nine outta ten times you're looking at somebody gettin' his throat slit open, or beat to a pulp with baseball bats and motorcycle chains. A gun ain't usually the weapon of choice. Too removed."

"You're saying you don't think the Demetros are responsible for the murders?"

"I'm saying' you gotta take everythin' into consideration, is all."

Munch nodded, rubbing his chin.

"If the feud between the Bashes and Demetros was reaching critical mass, wouldn't the *baro* have known about it?"

"Damn right, he would," Grogan said. "Especially around your neck of the woods."

"How's that?"

"You ever hearda Fat Louie Pulika?"

Munch shook his head.

"Well, he's your guy. A fuckin' prize character. Sly as a fox, but good for his word once you cut a deal with him . . . *if* you come to him through the right channels, and dealing with you happens to be in his interest. Otherwise he won't give you the time a' day."

"Such an unqualified recommendation," Munch mumbled under his breath.

"Huh?"

"Never mind," Munch waved his hand dismissively. "Say I want to talk to him. What's the right channel for me?"

"Not what. *Who*."

"Okay," Munch said. "Who."

"You're lookin' at him, sweetheart," Grogan said.

Munch didn't know why that surprised him.

"Can you arrange a meeting?"

Grogan shrugged. "I'll try. That is, providin' you pick up our dinner tab."

Munch reached for his wallet and slapped a few bills onto the table.

"Leavin' so soon?" Grogan asked. "You ain't hardly touched your food."

"Go ahead and finish it," Munch said. "I've got an early day tomorrow."

Grogan shrugged again, reached for Munch's plate and slid it in front of himself.

Munch buttoned his coat. As he was rising from his chair, his eye happened on the photo of the burning castle that was taped to the backbar.

"The bartender into history?" he asked.

Grogan regarded him inquisitively, already gobbling his secondhand meatballs.

Munch tipped his head toward the picture. "Looks like a scene from a World War II air raid or something."

"Oh, *that*." Grogan smiled. "No way, pal. You're looking at Windsor Castle, former weekend home to the Queen Mother of England—Elizabeth, the fuckin' *anus horriblis*. Day the place went up in flames was a winning occasion for us Irish, you ask me. It's just a shame Lizzie and her brood of royal pricks weren't there to get broiled with the furnishings."

Munch laughed, though he wasn't quite sure what the hell was so funny.

He put out his hand for Grogan to shake, said good-bye and threaded his way through the crowd to the entrance. At the bar the Champ took a last swipe at nothing at all before sinking headfirst to the countertop, his battle lost to a decision it was doubtful he remotely understood.

Munch watched him a moment from the door, then turned up his collar and dashed outside to his car.

THE NIGHT AFTER the murders Mihial Bash stayed up late drinking, and in that sense whiskey was his salvation from the fire.

The miraculous thing about it was that he almost never drank alone, and had tried going to bed stone-cold sober at about ten or eleven o'clock, long before he pulled the bottle of Cutty Sark off the shelf. But he'd been thinking about Alexei and Christine, and had lain there awake in the dark, unable to sleep, his mattress feeling too soft, his pillow too hard, had lain there staring up at the cracked, scarred ceiling and seen their faces drifting between pockets of shadow like the faces of restless ghosts. They had hovered above him, looking not as they had in life, but rather as they'd been when he'd walked into the *ofisa* and found them dead on the floor, their bodies twisted into impossible positions, the bright red smears on their faces making it appear as if they'd been weeping blood, Alexei sprawled on his back with one eye open in a look of mute accusation.

As the hours and minutes had crawled toward midnight, Mihial had switched on the bedside lamp and continued lying in its washed-out yellow light for quite a while before he finally kicked off his blankets and went downstairs. He'd been saving the Cutty Sark for a special occasion, a celebration, but instead he would open it for an event of a very different sort, drink it to numb his grief over the murders of his nephew and his nephew's wife, two people he'd loved, Alexei and Christine, gone now, shot to death in his own place of business.

And so he'd entered the room behind the front parlor, unfolded the card table he kept there, then sat behind it, the whiskey bottle on his left side, a tall glass on his right, and had himself a drink. A good, *stiff* drink, no water, no ice, nothing but the booze that he'd poured almost to the rim of the glass and drained in one long swallow. And then he'd poured another, and another. And somehow

69

each time he tilted the glass to his lips, it had felt as if *he* were emptying away instead of the booze, emptying into the glass, into the bottle, into a place where his backbreaking freight of guilt and sorrow might be lifted.

Maybe it wasn't his fault they had showed up just in time to be murdered, not directly, but he'd known what Vera and the girl were up to, known more or less about their plans, and had done nothing to stop them. Vera was his child, his daughter, and whether or not it would have done any good, he should have tried. Even as a little girl she'd been defiant, going off in her own direction, seeking out friends among the *gaje* against his early protestations, and later in spite of his most severe threats and punishments. Sometimes he wondered if he'd wished too much for a boy when his wife had gotten pregnant, if Vera's disregard for the old ways, her refusal to live as a Rom, was a kind of punishment for having felt himself unlucky at her birth. Or was it just that he was weak, and might that weakness have been the reason he'd been unable to produce a son in the first place?

He didn't know, and wasn't sure that it made a difference. All her life Vera had done as she'd pleased, to his lasting shame . . . and now that shame had spread, infected his clan like a curse or a sickness. He was the father, and he never should have let her have her way, not when she was a child, or the other day when she'd come from Washington to stick her nose in business she should have stayed out of. What he should have done was told her to stay where she'd gone to study her people as if they were dead things in a *gaje* museum. But he'd let his heart get the better of his head. And why? Why, though he'd known very well the trouble she would bring?

No, he couldn't deny his part in what happened. He was nearly as much to blame as his daughter and the girl.

As Mihial Bash had sat there at the card table slugging back drink after drink, all these thoughts had floated through his mind in a soporific wash, never quite leaving him, occasionally mixing with the anger and hatred he felt toward the Demetros, feelings that no amount of whiskey would obliterate—not if he drank one bottle or ten or a hundred, not if he robbed every liquor store in Baltimore of their stock and drowned himself in an endlessly flowing river of booze. Still, he had remained downstairs with his bottle and his glass and his rancid stew of emotions, and at some point in the night had found himself holding the wristwatch he'd discovered beside the bodies of Alexei and Christine, the wristwatch that had been the only proof he'd needed to confirm what he immediately suspected—that it was the Demetros who'd broken into the *ofisa,* that one of them had fired the bullets that killed his relatives.

Staring at the watch, Mihial had been unable to remember how it got there, unable to remember actually getting up from the card table, walking across the room and taking it from the desk drawer

71

where he'd hidden it away. It was as if it had appeared by magic, the same magic that the *gajes* were quick to mock when their lives were on track, and just as willing to believe in when their problems overcame them.

He'd held the watch, clutched it in his trembling hand, examining the side where the pin had snapped out of the band, and the band had come loose, causing it to fall off the wearer's wrist. He turned it facedown to read the initials inscribed in back, J.D., the killer's initials.

J.D.

Janos Demetro.

The eldest son of Al Demetro, a man who had been a source of constant trouble for the Bashes. Who had held a grudge against them for years. Who had repeatedly tainted them with his false accusations, and threatened to "squeeze out of him"— those had been his exact words when they'd last argued; Mihial could almost hear Al shouting them to his face along with his charges and evil wishes— the money he claimed was his.

"Te shorjdol mange rat amaro kuro," he'd said.

May your blood be spilled for my revenge.

He had used his son's hand to take his enemy's money, his son's hand to spill his enemy's blood . . . but he surely, surely hadn't expected that his guilt would be revealed by what his son's hand had left behind.

His thick fingers curled into a fist around the watch, his eyes bright with the force of his hatred, drunk but not drunk enough, Mihial was sitting there in the dimness, sitting there trying to decide what form his own revenge would take, when he heard the crash of breaking glass from the parlor, looked up to see the bottle rolling on the floor amid an avalanche of glittering shards and, even before he actually saw the fiery rag stuffed into the bottle's mouth, registered that somebody had tossed a Molotov cocktail through the window.

Shoving the watch into his pocket, he pushed up from his chair and moved toward the parlor. His head felt swollen and dense, his legs wooden, and he almost tripped over his own feet before managing to steady himself, then take, one, two, three steps forward, smelling the gasoline that had puddled on the floor under the rolling bottle, swaying as he fought the heavy lag of the whiskey.

In the minute it took to reach the parlor, Mihial had time to hear the screech of tires out in the street, and glimpse both the car speeding away from the curb near the *ofisa,* and the vanity license plate on the car's rear bumper. Then the gas in the bottle ignited with a hot, breathy *whoosh* and the crude incendiary bomb exploded, sending a shower of orange-yellow firedrops through the air. Flames slithered on the floor like angry snakes and then went leaping upward, coiling up the legs of the table supporting the crystal ball, climbing the back of the wicker chair, flashing hungrily as they set it ablaze.

Mihial looked around desperately for something he could use to beat out the fire, noticed a hanging rug to his left and tore the rug off the wall. Gripping it by the edges, he repeatedly swung it against the chair, battered the flames twisting up the chair back, slapped the rug over the flames until they were extinguished. His eyes watering, coughing from the blob of acrid smoke that had already risen toward the ceiling, he whirled around on his bare feet and swept the rug down the fiery torch that only seconds ago had been a table, blanketing its top with the thick woven fabric. Spatters of burning fuel singed the hairs on his bare arms and made tiny brown scorch marks on his T-shirt.

Mihial looked around to see if anything else had caught fire, saw a churning pool of flame on the floor where the bottle had shattered, and rushed over to put it out. Jagged splinters of glass hooked into his feet as he stood swatting the flames with the rug, oblivious to the stench of his own searing flesh as the fire ravished him with its dying licks.

Then finally it was out, and there was only the dark smoke spiraling out the broken window into the night. Gasping raggedly, he sank to his knees, his hands already red and pulsing from his burns.

Mihial bowed his head and emitted a high, choked moan, tears of pain and impotent rage spilling from his eyes, leaving wet tracks on both his cheeks.

Demetro, it had been Demetro again, and this time he had wanted Mihial to know.

He wiped his eyes and looked out at the street, heard the shriek of fire trucks bouncing from building to building. His thoughts and emotions had been compressed into a single word, a single *name,* turning and turning in his head as if on a nonstop tape loop.

Demetro, Demetro, Demetro.

He had done his work, and now Mihial would do his own.

SIX

ALTHOUGH PEMBLETON'S SHIFT did not begin until eight A.M.—in fact, roll call for the detectives was at eight-forty—he was in the squad room at seven-thirty on Tuesday, the second day of the Bash probe, eager to get a jump on the morning. The first forty-eight hours of a murder investigation were the most critical in terms of gathering evidence and developing leads, and thus far Pembleton felt he'd made insufficient headway on both fronts.

As he came over to his desk, he saw a scrawled note from Bayliss in his memo tray, sending his regards, adding that he hoped Frank and Munch were still behaving themselves, and, last but not least, giving him the phone number of a fire department investigator who'd called in connection with Pembleton's Gypsy investigation.

Pembleton couldn't imagine what that connection might be, but figured he'd return the call right away, and was reaching for the telephone on his desk when Munch's extension began trilling across the room.

Munch had not yet arrived at headquarters, and Pembleton looked over at his vacant desk, debating whether he should take the call, something he'd have done automatically had it been Bayliss's phone that was ringing. After a moment he realized he was being thick, lifted his handset and punched up Munch's blinking line.

"Baltimore City Homicide, Detective Pembleton speaking."

"Pembleton?"

"Yes."

"Where the hell's Munch?"

Pembleton held the phone away from his ear. The caller sounded as if he were shouting through wet cotton.

"He isn't in yet," he said. "Do you want to leave him a mess—"

"You his partner?"

"Yes." Pembleton almost added the word *temporarily,* but caught himself.

"Thought he mentioned you once or twice."

Pembleton's brow furrowed with interest. "May I ask who's calling?"

"Harry Grogan."

Pembleton searched his memory a moment, then placed the name with a mental click of recognition. Grogan. The Gypsy expert working out of Western.

"You have anything for us?" he asked, knowing

Munch had planned to meet with Grogan the previous night.

"I'd rather talk to Munch," Grogan said. "If you don't mind."

Pembleton glanced at his wristwatch.

"He ought to be here any minute," he said. "But if this is important—"

"It's real important," Grogan interrupted.

"Then maybe you'd better talk to me."

"Well, I dunno."

"What's the problem?" Pembleton said.

"I just don't want to blow anything."

" 'Blow' anything?"

"Right."

"For who?"

"For you," Grogan said. "*Or* me."

Silence. Pembleton wondered why Grogan was being so mysterious, decided he was too busy to trouble himself about it.

"Have it your way," he said. "I'll pass along your message."

"Wait a minute," Grogan said.

"Yes?"

"Why you givin' me the bum's rush?"

"Look, Grogan, you're the one who doesn't want to talk—"

"It ain't a question of *wanting*—"

"Or can't talk, or whatever," Pembleton said. "I'm in the middle of a double murder investigation, and if you have info you'd like to share, fine. If not, that's also okay with me."

"Hey, I didn't mean to offend you—"

"I'm not offended."

"Get you pissed off, then," Grogan said. "Besides, I never said I absolutely *wouldn't* talk to you. It's just that me an' Munch already know each other, and what I'm callin' about is kinda sensitive."

Pembleton guiltily reached for his cigarettes. Over breakfast Mary had praised his efforts to cut back and showed him the latest magazine article she'd clipped on the ill effects of secondary smoke. Every time you have a cigarette in the house, the baby might as well be smoking it with you, she'd reminded him, flashing a smile that she usually reserved for winning arguments or talking him into expensive purchases.

Well, this isn't my house, he thought, and lit up.

"Too bad you couldn't make it yesterday, by the way," Grogan said. "We had a nice time."

"Glad to hear it," Pembleton said. He took his first drag and felt his nerves unwind with a grateful sigh. "You ready to give me the information yet?"

"Ah, why not?" Grogan said. "We're all cops, ain't we?"

Pembleton blew a series of smoke rings and watched them float toward the ceiling.

"All right," Grogan said. "When we got done talkin' last night, I told Munch I'd try an' arrange a little sit-down between him and the local *baro*."

"The local what?"

"*Baro.*" Grogan harrumphed wetly. "See, this is why I wanted Munch. Not that I'm goin' back on talkin' to *you*, understand. It's just that he's already familiar with certain things havin' to do with Gypsies."

"Good-bye," Pembleton said brusquely.

"Okay, okay, here's the scoop. A *baro*'s a Gypsy honcho, a combination judge, social worker, power broker—"

"A man of influence," Pembleton said, moving him along.

"You're a quick learner," Grogan said. "Around Baltimore, the *baro* happens to be a guy named Fat Louie Pulika."

"And . . . ?"

"And I already asked him if he'd be willin' to have a palaver with Munch, and he said 'sure.' Which kinda surprised me."

"Because Gypsies aren't usually very communicative when it comes to cops."

"Like I said, you're a bright guy."

"He give you specific time for the meeting?"

"Yeah. Tonight at twelve."

"*Midnight?*"

"What can I say? These people keep late hours," Grogan told him. "I wouldn't bitch about it too much, though. Pulika could be a big help."

Pembleton frowned, already wondering how to tell his wife he'd be leaving the house when it was his turn to take care of the baby. But he couldn't very well expect Munch to work the case on his own time without doing the same himself. Additionally, Pulika was—as Grogan had suggested—a vital contact, and, rightly or wrongly, he wasn't comfortable trusting Munch to make that contact alone.

"All right," Pembleton said. "You got a place to go with the time?"

"If you get a pen to go with a piece of paper," Grogan said.

FORTY MINUTES LATER Pembleton was back at the scene of the crime, following up on what he'd learned from his callback to the fire department investigator—namely that there had been a fire at Mihial Bash's fortune-telling joint at about three o'clock that morning, that the investigator suspected arson and that his preliminary cross-checks had made him aware of a BCPD shooting call at the same location within the past twenty-four hours.

Pembleton had thanked the fire cop for his tip and left headquarters almost immediately, leaving Munch his destination in a hastily written note, and asking him to talk to the people living in the apartment building where Alexei and Christine Bash had worked as supers, in case they knew anything of consequence about the victims or the daughter they'd supposedly left behind.

"Like a stinking icebox in here, ain't it?" Mihial Bash said.

He was standing on a ladder in his storefront, hanging transparent plastic sheeting over the yawning space that had been his display window. Both of his hands were bandaged.

Pembleton steamed his fingers with his breath.

"Yeah," he said. "It's cold."

"Heat'll stay in better once I'm done covering up this hole," Bash said.

Pembleton watched him thump down on an industrial stapler to attach the top corner of the sheeting to the window frame. The trace odors of smoke and gasoline were making Pembleton's nostrils smart and his eyes grainy, adding to the discomfort he felt due to the room's low temperature.

"Mr. Bash, can you tell me what happened here this morning?" he asked.

"I had a fire," Bash said.

Pembleton sighed. He hadn't really expected more.

"That's it?"

"Uh-huh."

"You know how it started?" Pembleton asked.

"Sure," Bash said. "I got drunk and knocked over an oil lamp. Stupid accident."

"An oil lamp?"

"Right."

"You usually use that instead of the electric lights?"

"When I'm trying to relax. I was laying in bed awhile and couldn't sleep. Thinking about my cousin and his wife, you know. Figured a shot of whiskey would calm me down."

"So you came downstairs for a drink?"

"Wound up having a lot more than one," he said. "I was pretty upset."

Pembleton nodded his head toward the broken window.

"What about that?"

"The lamp was on the table where we kept the crystal ball. I bumped into the table and it fell over and smashed against the window. The lamp must've landed on its side and spilled oil all over the floor."

Pembleton wondered how long it had taken Bash to prepare that recital.

"Goddamn hands hurt," Bash complained under his breath, punching in another staple.

Pembleton looked up at him. "As I remember, the table wasn't very big. But you're saying it tipped over and smashed a *plate glass* window?"

"Crazy fluke, ain't it," Bash said. "You should've heard my insurance agent when I told him the story over the phone."

Pembleton kept looking at him.

"Did you usually burn gasoline in the lamp? Because that's what I smell."

Bash sniffed the air theatrically.

"Smells like lamp oil to me," he said. "Which is what it was."

Pembleton stood there quietly a moment, thinking about how to proceed.

"I spoke to an arson investigator this morning," he said at last. "He believed the fire to be suspicious in origin."

"What can I say?" Bash held an edge of the

84

plastic sheeting steady against the window frame and stapled it down. "I'm telling you the truth."

"Mr. Bash, my department's investigation takes precedence over any other that may be pending, but I can see to it that an arson squad turns this place inside out. I'm trying to give you a chance here."

Bash said nothing.

Pembleton shifted his weight on the sooty, blackened floorboards. The broom used to sweep away the broken window glass had missed a few splinters and they gritted under his shoes.

"Why haven't you told me your nephew had a child?" he said.

Pembleton was watching Bash carefully for a reaction, and he got one. Bash straightened up as if he'd received a mild jolt of current.

"Nobody asked," he said.

"My partner and I spoke to you, your daughter *and* your mother yesterday. Don't any of you think that's something the police should know?"

"Well, I don't see what Alexei and Christine being parents has to do with them getting killed."

"With all due respect, sir, it's *my* job to determine if there's a connection."

"Well, so now you know about Carmen," Bash said. "Don't see what difference it'll make."

"Carmen? Is that her name?"

Bash's left cheek quivered for a split second. Pembleton guessed he was angry at himself for letting something slip.

"Is that her name?" he repeated.

"Yeah," Bash said.

Pembleton nodded.

"How old is she?"

Bash shrugged. "Maybe fourteen."

"Uh-huh," Pembleton said, reaching into his pocket for his notepad. "And can you tell me where she is right now?"

Bash went silent.

"Mr. Bash . . ."

"I don't know."

Pembleton continued pressing him. "We have a teenage girl whose parents, your relatives, were murdered yesterday. Shot to death not fifteen feet from where we're standing. Shot to death while they were visiting you. But you expect me to believe you don't know where to find her."

"What I meant was, I don't know *exactly*." Bash said, backpedaling.

"Then give me a rough idea."

Bash stared at him with his opaque black eyes.

"I think she's with one of Christine's sisters," he said.

"*One* of them?"

"Yeah."

"How many sisters does she have?"

"I'm not sure. Four, five."

"And which one are we talking about?"

"I'm not sure. Svieta, probably."

"Where's Svieta live?"

"Best I can remember, somewhere out around Newbury."

"Does Svieta have a second name?"

"I couldn't tell you what it is. We hardly know each other."

"What about Lovera?" Pembleton said, seeing a perfect chance to mention Bash's daughter. "Would she have that information?"

"I doubt it," Bash said. "Look, maybe you haven't noticed, but I got work to do—"

"Mr. Bash, if you don't mind, I'd like to ask Lovera a question or two."

"I'm telling you, she wouldn't be any help. Besides, she's not home."

"When will she be back?"

"I dunno. Tonight maybe."

"Fine." Pembleton's eyes had remained fixed on Bash's. "Please have her call me or my partner, Detective Munch, as soon as possible."

"All right."

"*Before* she returns to Washington."

"All right."

"I appreciate it," Pembleton said, gearing up for another fastball. "And Mr. Bash . . . ?"

"Yeah?"

"Do you happen to know what year Mustang Vera owns?"

Bash's shoulders jolted up straight again, except this time there was nothing mild about his surprise. This time he looked like he'd touched the live end of a mainline power cable.

"No," he said, shaking his head agitatedly.

Pembleton held Bash's gaze another moment and

then put away his pad, satisfied he'd hit him in the right spot. The man was not merely being evasive when it came to his daughter, he seemed outright frightened.

"I'll ask Lovera about the car when she calls," Pembleton said.

And swept out the door with Bash staring after him from atop his ladder.

307 BELVEDERE PLACE was a five-story pile of bricks fronted by a narrow courtyard and facing a grim line of row houses across the street. The wind had overturned a trash can near the sagging entry doors, and a cheap, discarded print of the Nativity lay amid the other rubbish like a tainted miracle. The snow crusting the unshoveled walks was trampled and sooty.

After knocking on almost every door on the ground floor, Munch still hadn't struck paydirt. The tenants either weren't home or wanted him to think they weren't. Nobody had answered in the first four apartments he'd tried, and a spyglass opening and shutting in the fifth door had been the closest he'd gotten to any sign of life.

The last apartment Munch stopped at before heading upstairs was 1G. He knocked, waited a minute and was starting to turn away when he heard the sound of shuffling feet followed by the metallic rattle of tumblers.

"Who is it?" a man said, opening the door a crack and peering out from under a night chain.

Munch flashed his shield.

"Detective Munch, Baltimore City Homicide."

"Whoa. Just a minute."

The door closed, the chain was unlatched, the door reopened, and an old guy in a T-shirt, boxer shorts and slippers appeared.

"Whoa," he repeated. His wrinkled face looked like a walnut. "Somebody get killed?"

"Are you acquainted with Alexei and Christine Bash?"

"Sure," the guy said. "The super and his wife. *They* got killed?"

"I'm afraid so."

"When it happen?"

"The night before last. Sir—"

"No wonder the building looks like shit," the old man blurted. "You seen that spilled garbage out front? It's a *pigsty.*"

"Sir, may I please have your name," Munch said, taking out his pad

"Mal. Mal Sayers."

"Mr. Sayers, I just have a few brief questions."

"Hey, sure."

"When was last time you saw the Bashes?"

"Today's Friday, right?"

"Tuesday, sir."

Sayers screwed up his face.

"You positive?"

Munch nodded.

"Well, then it was Sunday afternoon when I saw Alexei." The old man reached a hand behind his back, slipped it well below the waistband of his shorts and scratched. "*Had* to have been Sunday, come to think."

"How's that?"

"Because he only cleaned the building on weekends. Hallways were Saturdays, stairs were Sundays. I remember telling him to put some *wax* on those damn steps, but he didn't listen."

"Wax?"

"Sure. Gives 'em a nice shine."

Munch wondered if many people waxed their stairs. To him that made about as much sense as paving a highway with glass, or stuffing a pillow with razor wire . . . but what did he know about building maintenance?

"Did you have any conversation with him? Besides what you've just mentioned."

Sayer shook his head. "He *worked* here. We weren't friends."

"What's that mean?"

"Means he didn't wax the stairs. To me that's lazy, and I hate lazy. Plus we have waterbugs crawling up from the cellar." Still scratching himself with one hand, Sayer held up the other and spread its thumb and pointer finger two inches apart. "Big ones. You'd think the guy could've laid some traps."

"Getting back to Sunday," Munch said. "Was Mr. Bash's behavior at all out of the ordinary?"

"Nope."

"How about his wife? Did you also see her that afternoon?"

The old man shrugged. "I might've passed her in the hall."

"Sir," Munch said, "can you tell me if the Bashes had a teenage daughter?"

"A disgraceful *brat*'s what I'd call her."

Munch looked at him. "Why's that?"

"Because she had no respect for her parents, that's why. Always fighting with them."

"You *witnessed* them fighting?"

"Right," Sayer said. "She'd slam out of their apartment, and they'd end up shouting at each other in the lobby."

"By 'they' do you mean that both parents would be involved in these episodes?"

"Sometimes one, sometimes both."

"By the way," Munch said, "do you happen to know the daughter's name?"

"No. Should I?"

Munch didn't answer. He'd never quite come to understand the kick people get out of giving cops a hard time.

"Is *she* the killer?" Sayer asked.

"Our investigation's just started," Munch replied noncommittally. "Sir, when they fought . . . do you have any idea what the arguments were about?"

Sayer gave him an indignant frown. "You think I'm some kind of eavesdropper?"

"All I'm asking, since you did state that you heard them arguing loudly on several occasions, is

91

what they might have said to each other," Munch said. "To the best of your knowledge."

"I didn't pay attention."

"You can't recall *anything*?"

Sayer hesitated a moment. "Well, let me think." He pulled his hand out of his underpants and switched to scratching his head. "A couple times they were yelling about school."

Munch looked at him again.

"School?"

"Like I said, I didn't pay much attention. Figured she was sneaking out of class to run around with boys. You ought to see the pants she wears, ain't nothing but tights. Like the kind that belong in a gymnasium."

"How do you know?"

"Hey, I might be old, but these eyes still work fine—"

"I meant about her cutting class. Did you actually overhear any comments to that effect?"

"Didn't need to," Sayer declared. "Those truant officers were always coming around, asking lots of questions, and being cagey about why they were asking 'em. Same way you're being cagey with me."

"Did they ever speak to you personally?"

"Yeah, and I told 'em what I'm telling you. That I mind my own business."

"Uh-huh," Munch said wearily.

The old man examined the finger he'd been

scratching himself with, then held it to his nose and sniffed it analytically.

"Can I get back to Regis and Kathie Lee now?" he said.

"In a minute," Munch said. "About the daughter . . . could you describe her for me?"

"Thin. Long black hair. Already told you how she dressed. I guess you'd say she was pretty for one of those dark-skinned types."

"Anything else?"

Sayer shook his head.

"And when did you last see her?"

"Hmmm. See or *hear*?"

"Either one, sir. The last time you were aware of her presence."

"Well, I heard her storm outta the house the night before last."

"Around what time was that?"

"I don't know. Nine-thirty, ten o'clock."

No more than eight hours before the murders, Munch thought.

"Go on," he said.

"Ain't much to tell you. I was getting ready to turn in when the super's door bangs open really loud and out she comes. She's carrying on, getting all pissy—"

"She was crying?"

Sayer nodded. "Sounded like it to me. Bet she wanted to go gallivanting around instead of doing her homework."

Munch sighed, trying to recall when he'd last heard someone actually use the word *gallivanting*.

"Could you make out anything she said?"

"Hey, I might be old, but these ears still work fine," Sayer said.

Which, since he'd already assured Munch of his visual acuity, left only his senses of taste, touch and smell unvouched for.

"And . . . ?" Munch said encouragingly.

"And what the girl told her parents was that she didn't need 'em anymore. That she finally had somebody who was on her side."

"Were those her exact words?"

"Yessir. Or real close." Sayer paused. "She was probably talking about a boyfriend, eh?"

Munch stood there in silence. Chances were that Sayer was right about the causes of the friction between the girl and her parents. Boys, school . . . teenagers were teenagers. On the other hand, something the old guy'd said had sparked a recollection, and suddenly made him wonder if the arguments might be placed in an altogether different context.

"Mr. Sayer, did you ever see the girl with anyone besides her mother and father?"

"No."

"Are you sure? Please think back."

Sayer shook his head vehemently. "Hey, I ain't senile yet!"

Munch inhaled, exhaled and closed his pad.

"That's it for now, Mr. Sayer. Thank you very much."

"Don't mention it," Sayer grumbled, then hitched up his shorts and shut the door in Munch's face.

THE NEXT TENANT Munch questioned turned out to be an even more thunderous geyser of complaint than Sayers. Eleanore Lembock, apartment 2E, was a short, stooped woman in her seventies who had carrot-colored hair and wore a pink print house-dress. The collar of the housedress was unbuttoned and had flapped back to reveal raging blooms of eczema below her neck. Glops of medicinal-smelling cream floated over the inflamed, broken skin like steam over a volcanic eruption.

After expressing her shock and disbelief over the murders—Munch wondered if anybody in the building read the *Sun,* which had reported the story on page three of the previous day's edition—Mrs. Lembock launched into an unsparing critique of Alexei Bash's performance as building superinten-dent, citing as her particular gripes his slowness to repair a drippy faucet in her bathtub and an occa-sionally leaking pipe under her sink, his inattention when she'd reported the hiss in her toilet tank that acted up every other Sunday at five A.M., his irritating habit of sending up too much heat during the day and not enough at night and his refusal to impose a blanket ban on deliveries from Chinese restaurants, something she'd been after him to do for a year.

"That funny food stinks up the halls," she ex-plained, offering Munch a snaggle-toothed smile.

"By the way, you want to come in and have some Sanka?"

Munch peered into her darkened foyer and declined.

"Mrs. Lembock," he said, "do you know of any arguments the Bashes may have been having with their daughter? I was told she—"

"A horrible, *horrible* girl," she said. "Her name's Carmen, like the opera. I think."

Munch held his pen ready over his notebook. "You think?"

"Well, it's either that or Charmin. Like the toilet paper."

He jotted both names down, putting question marks beside them.

"Is there a specific reason you feel she's so awful?"

"Those fights you mentioned, for one thing. She would stand in the lobby and shout at her parents."

"Do you remember what the shouting was about?"

"No," she said. "I'd hear their voices, you know, but up here on the second floor it was hard to hear what they were saying. Not that I'm the type to listen in."

"Ma'am," Munch said, "if you don't know why they were fighting, how can you be absolutely certain the daughter was at fault?"

"Because mothers are right no matter *what,*" she proclaimed. "And believe me, Christina was the only good one in the bunch."

"Why do you say that?"

96

"Well, she gave me wonderful advice."

Munch's attention perked.

"What sort?"

Mrs. Lembock's expression suddenly became veiled.

"Are you sure you wouldn't like a cup of coffee?" she asked, and smoothed a lump of ointment over the raw skin on her chest.

"No, thanks," Munch said. "What sort of advice do you mean?"

"Gypsy advice." That guarded look was still on her face. "Did I do anything illegal by paying for it?"

"No, ma'am," Munch said, keeping quiet about his suspicions that Christine Bash had violated the law by *accepting* payment. Though he was no Harry Grogan when it came to being up on Gypsy activities, he knew Baltimore had strict licensing codes regulating fortune-tellers, as well as a civil ordinance prohibiting the dual usage of ground-floor spaces as professional and residential quarters.

"You know," Mrs. Lembock said, reassured of her own honesty, "Christine charged ten dollars a session, but they were worth every cent."

"Can you be a little more specific about her services?"

"Sure." She bared her crooked teeth in a grin of delight. "I'll give you a *demonstration.*"

She shot out a hand that was as red as a lobster claw, grabbed his wrist and twisted it around before

97

he could pull away. His pen went clattering to the floor.

"You can pick it up in a minute," she said. "Right off I can see you're a morbid person."

"How's that?" Munch was hoping her skin rash wasn't contagious.

"Your middle finger's crooked," she said.

"Oh."

"This here's your lifeline," Mrs. Lembock said, running a fingertip down his palm. "Uh-oh."

"What's wrong?"

"Well, it ends in a cross."

"Is that bad?"

"Better skip it," she said. "Your fate line shows a happy marriage anyway."

"I'm divorced."

"Maybe your second marriage—"

"*Twice* divorced," he said.

"Well," she said, abruptly letting go of him and returning his pen. "I'd better leave this kind of thing to the Gypsies."

"Ma'am, how long had you been getting palm readings from Christine Bash?"

"I really couldn't—"

"Approximately."

She shrugged. "Since maybe a month after her husband took over as super. I suppose that'd make it almost a year."

"And how often did you have these sessions?"

"About once a week," she said.

Munch looked at her. At ten dollars a pop, that came to quite a bit of cash.

"If you don't mind, Mrs. Lemlock, could you explain how you were approached about the readings?"

"One of them slipped a little pamphlet under my door."

"Did all the tenants get pamphlets?"

"I couldn't say."

Munch was willing to bet the solicitation had been limited to tenants judged unlikely to report it to the landlord—who he doubted had listed palmistry among Bash's job specs.

"By one of them, you mean either Christine or Alexei . . . ?"

"No," she said, looking as if his question had been somehow idiotic. "Christine or the *girl*. Only Gypsy women have an occult nature; the men don't get involved."

How unenlightened of me, Munch thought dryly.

"Did you ever actually see Christine's daughter with the pamphlets."

"Yes. Well, maybe not in the building. But I saw her handing them out to people plenty of times."

"People on the street?"

"Yes."

"Was it during the day or night?"

"What?" she asked.

"Was it during the day or night?" he repeated.

"Daytime," she said. "I do my grocery shopping

and such in the morning, so that I'm home in time for my story. And I never go out after dark."

"Was it a *week*day?"

"Young man, you're asking me to remember quite a bit—"

"Please try."

"Well. . . ." Her face scrunched up in thought. "For a while I think it was *every* day. Because, you know, she'd be standing on the corner whenever I left the house. Since all the arguing started, I haven't noticed her out there as much."

"Mrs. Lembock, have you seen the girl in the past forty-eight hours?"

"No."

"Did you ever see her with anyone other than her parents?"

"You mean like a boyfriend?"

"Anybody at all."

"No. No, I haven't."

Munch snapped his notepad shut.

"Finally, ma'am, would you happen to have one of those handbills laying around? If you do, I'd like to take a look at it."

"Well, I can check my dresser drawer," she said. "The top one's where I keep important papers."

"That'd be great," Munch said.

"Would you like to come in while I look? I can still put up water for the Sanka—"

Munch watched her peel a flake of dry ointment off her chest.

"I'll wait out here, thank you," he said.

• • •

GABRIELLA REYES LIVED in apartment 5F with her infant daughter and two sleek black-and-white tuxedo cats. Pretty, pleasant and in her mid-twenties, she told Munch that she worked as a night nurse at Baltimore Central and had neither seen nor heard any of the shouting matches between the battling Bashes. She had, however, received one of Christine's pamphlets under her door when she'd first moved into the building six months back.

"I was kinda amazed," she said, standing in her doorway and burping the tiny, pink-bundled infant in her arms.

"Why's that?" Munch asked.

She shrugged a little. "Not many supers double as fortune-tellers."

"I see your point," Munch said. "What did you do about the pamphlet?"

"Before or after I tossed it?" she said. "Detective, I work with *cancer* patients. People who are terminally ill. These readers, they take advantage of people's suffering, you know? Makes me sick." The baby gurgled and hiccuped. "Christine and her husband, they probably figured I was an easy mark. Single mother, Hispanic, I don't need to spell it out. For half my paycheck they'd have told me Zorro's gonna ride up on a white horse and sweep me off to his Mexican villa."

Munch laughed. One of the cats came slinking out into the hall and rubbed against his ankle.

"Fayard, get back inside," she said.

"Fayard?" Munch bent and scratched the purring cat behind its ear. "Interesting name for a kitty."

"His brother's Howard. Like the Nicholas Brothers. They're—"

"The greatest hoofers of all time," Munch said.

She grinned. "Yeah. These cats remind me of them. The graceful way they move. And the tuxedo markings."

Munch straightened up.

"Miss Reyes—"

"Gabriella."

"Gabriella," he said. "You said you hadn't heard the fights Alexei and Christina had been having with their daughter. But can you tell me anything at all about the girl?"

"Not much," she said. "Carmen's a sweet, shy kid—"

"That's the daughter's name? You're positive?"

"Sure. We've talked a few times."

"About what?"

"Mostly she asks me what it's like working as a nurse, being a mother, being on my own, that sort of thing. She always seems very sad."

Munch looked at her. "Has she ever told you she was unhappy living with her parents?"

"Not in so many words. But it wasn't that long ago I was her age. You pick up on certain things."

"Did you ever see her handing out fliers for her mother?"

Gabriella nodded. "A real shame, you ask me. She'd dress up in gold hoop earrings and a Gypsy skirt, like she just got here from the old country. Far as I know, she never wore those clothes when she wasn't out there on the corner."

"*Then* how would she dress?"

"Like any other normal teenager. Jeans, spandex, loud sneakers . . ." She shifted the baby from one shoulder to the other. "Believe me, Detective Munch, the poor kid wanted out."

"From her folks?"

"From being forced to do things she didn't want to do."

Munch was silent a moment. Fayard and Howard were both out in the hall now, taking turns bounding and somersaulting over each other, doing flawless imitations of their namesakes. Gabriella Reyes shifted her wriggling pink bundle again.

"I'll only keep you another second," Munch said.

"Appreciate it. Squirt here feels like she's getting heavier."

Munch smiled. "Gabriella, have you ever seen Carmen Bash hanging out with anybody?"

Gabriella shook her head.

"No friends?"

"No," she said. "Sorry."

"What about dating? Might she have confided in you about boys?"

"No, I'd definitely remember something like that," Gabriella said. "Only person she's ever mentioned is a cousin."

Munch's eyes narrowed behind his lenses.

"What did she say about him?"

103

"Well, actually, it's a *her*," Gabriella said. Once or twice Carmen said we were kind of alike . . . the cousin and me, that is. The way she seemed to be impressed with this person, I took it as a compliment."

"Did she tell you her cousin's name?"

"No," Gabriella said.

"Anything about her at all?"

"I don't think so. . . . Well, wait a minute."

"Yes?" Munch was still looking at her.

"I could be wrong—this was months ago—but I think Carmen said she was a teacher."

Munch stared at Gabriella and said nothing. He felt a sudden band of tightness across his upper back.

She regarded him curiously. "The cousin, could it be Carmen's run off with her?"

"I don't know," he said, and slipped his pad into his pocket. "But maybe I'd better find out."

SEVEN

TO BCPD AUTO theft cops, the drab, multi-acre sprawl of decaying warehouses between Fell's Point and Inner Harbor's artificial shine is known as Chop City, a street-smart variation on the phrase Charm City, which holds as Baltimore's official nickname, and has itself become bitterly ironic to the ghetto residents, who can only presume it was acquired before the charm became tarnished by drugs, poverty and governmental corruption, and the city's violent crime rate soared to the present high of nearly eight thousand incidents of murder, rape, theft and arson a year.

Day or night, summer or winter, the majority of times a vehicle is stolen in Baltimore's urban grid it winds up in Chop City, stripped, gutted and abandoned by thieves like a skeleton thoroughly picked over by carrion. The cops know it, the victims know it, the criminals know it. Whenever some poor slob reports his car missing, the cops will generally begin searching for it there among the filthy gutters and boarded-up buildings that run for block after block after block, each more desolate than the last.

As Pembleton and Munch drove through this forsaken part of town, their car bouncing torment-edly over the icy, pockmarked road, they found themselves wondering whether to praise or damn Harry Grogan for giving them the lowdown on Albert Demetro, patriarch of the Demetro clan. According to Grogan, Chop City was where Dem-etro owned—if not in name then by proxy—a notorious and nameless chop *shop,* which was both a one-stop for stolen auto parts and the command center for his many other shadowy business opera-tions.

Though they were well into the second day of the Bash investigation, and had spent that entire morn-ing doing wearisome legwork, neither detective had the slightest idea whether Demetro had anything to do with the shootings, Mihial Bash's accusations notwithstanding. In fact, as far as Pembleton was concerned, Lovera Bash was the only person whose behavior in the hours surrounding the murders raised significant questions. He had not yet told Munch what he'd learned from his latest visit with Mihial Bash, or mentioned their conversation at all, for that matter. For his own part, Munch had kept silent about his own suspicions that Lovera was hiding the victims' daughter for reasons that might or might not be tied into their killings. Each of the detectives, however, had promised himself that he would share his information with the other when they finally sat down to eat lunch after interviewing Demetro.

"At the peril of our lives must we bring home our bread," Pembleton said now, pointing out his window.

"Book of Job," Munch replied from the driver's seat.

Pembleton looked impressed.

"Does that sage quote mean we've reached Castle Demetro?" Munch said.

"Yeah," Pembleton said.

"Thought so," Munch said, and pulled to the right.

The garage was a bland concrete structure squatting on a lot filled with cars in various stages of disassembly. The half-raised door to the garage was made of corrugated aluminum and splashed with graffiti. Visible in the bay were several more vehicles, one of which was jacked up on lifts and being worked on by a mechanic in soiled blue coveralls.

The detectives drove into the lot, stopped the car and went toward the office. There was a soft drink machine to the right of the office door, a mound of jumbled tires to the left. Pembleton paused by the soft drink machine, slotted three quarters and pushed the button for a cola. A can of grape soda dropped out. He frowned, removed it from the dispenser and walked into the office with Munch.

The big man behind the desk heard the door open and jerked his head up from the daily racing form.

"Who're you?" he said.

"Baltimore City Homicide," Pembleton said, showing his badge and identification.

The guy read the ID with bleary eyes.

"Ain't nobody been killed around here," he said. "What d'you want?"

"To return this soda, for starters," Pembleton said, and banged the can down hard on the desktop. "I wanted a Coke."

"Here's your money back with interest." The big guy took a dollar bill from his pocket and flipped it across the desk. "What else can I do for you?"

"Tell Al Demetro we want to ask him a few questions," Pembleton said.

The big man's shoulders squared. "He's busy."

"We can wait till he isn't," Pembleton said. "This is pretty serious."

"Might be busy all day," the big man said.

"Fine," Munch said. "That gives us lotsa time to poke around the garage, check out the spare parts you're using."

"Go right ahead," the guy said.

"Be interesting if any of those parts has a serial number on it," Pembleton said to Munch.

"Especially if the number turns out to match a car on the latest stolen vehicle listing," Munch said. "Shall I radio in for it?"

"Might as well," Pembleton said.

Munch turned at once toward the door.

"Waitaminnit," the big guy said. "I can try an'

108

buzz Mr. Demetro in the back office. He ain't gonna like it, though."

"Can't imagine why," Munch said. "We're just a pair of friendly visitors who happen to be law enforcement officers."

The big guy scowled, reached across for the phone console and jabbed the intercom button.

A staticky voice blurted something incomprehensible from the speaker. To Pembleton it sounded like "Squarrkbool!"

"I got two murder cops here wanna talk to Mr. Demetro," the big man said, leaning over the console. "I told 'em he was busy but they say it's important."

There was another crackling burst of sound.

"The boss says he can make a little time for you," the big man told the detectives. He jutted his chin toward a door to one side of the desk. "Go through there into the garage, an' then walk to the back. You'll see another door says 'Office.' Somebody'll let you in."

"Thanks," Pembleton said.

"It's something the way you interpret the squawk from that intercom, fella," Munch said. "One day you'll have to show me how it's done."

The big man eyed him belligerently.

"Or maybe not," Munch said, and followed Pembleton through the door.

The garage stank of metal and motor oil. On the floor near the lifts, a small electric room heater was coughing out lukewarm air that did little to moderate the chill. The breath steamed from the mechanic's mouth as he attacked the jacked-up car with a lug wrench.

Pembleton and Munch strode to the door at the rear of the garage and waited, hands in their coat pockets. After a couple of minutes the door was swung open by a dark-haired guy with a face like a switchblade. He stood briefly in the middle of the entrance, looking the detectives over, then moved aside to let them through.

They stepped into what was, Pembleton guessed, a prefabricated addition to the garage. The room was long and narrow like the interior of a trailer. The floor was covered end to end by thick maroon carpeting. Mirrored panels on one wall reflected the glow from overhead fluorescents and gave the air a faint blue cast. Against the mirrored wall was a small bar with some stools around it. Two guys sat there drinking, a checkerboard between them on the Formica countertop. Both wore dark sports jackets and a lot of gold rings and had bright silk scarves flaring from the open collars of their shirts. One of them had on a floppy wide-brimmed hat that would have looked perfect on a street fiddler in Bucharest.

"A social club behind a seedy garage in one of the most rundown parts of town," Munch whispered to Pembleton. "This is what I call doing it à la ritz."

The detectives started forward. In back of the room was a fleecy maroon sofa flanked by a matching pair of armchairs. On the chair to the right of the couch was a lean guy of about twenty with longish black hair that had been combed straight back and gelled in place. He wore designer jeans and a white turtleneck and a wristwatch with an enormous gold band. The large-screen television in front of the sofa was tuned to a daytime quiz show. The man on the sofa with the remote in his hand had a wide jowly face, bushy eyebrows that almost met above the nose, and an electric mane of silver hair. He was smoking a cigar and, like the checker players, wore a silk scarf and a great many rings. No jacket, though.

His eyes slid from the TV to his visitors.

"I'm Al Demetro," he said. "What've you got on your minds?"

Pembleton and Munch walked by the two guys at the bar, who momentarily suspended their game and cranked their heads around to watch them. They were trying hard to strike a tough pose.

"We're looking into the murders of two people named Alexei and Christine Bash," Pembleton said.

"Who?"

Pembleton repeated their names.

"What makes you think I got any idea who they are?"

"My information is that you're pretty well acquainted with the Bash clan," Pembleton said.

"Well, your information sucks." Demetro shrugged and blew a plume of smoke. "You have the scoop on every black person in Baltimore, Detective?"

Out the corner of his eye Pembleton saw Bucharest grin, revealing a pair of golden incisors that harmonized neatly with his rings.

"That a rhetorical question?" he asked Demetro.

"I don't get what you mean."

"Here are some examples," Pembleton said. "What would happen if somebody went over *every one* of your garage's operating permits to make sure they're up to date?"

Demetro frowned around his cigar.

"Or if I were to arrange for the auto theft squad to keep this place under surveillance *every hour* of the day?"

Demetro's frown deepened.

"Or have *every* fortune-telling joint in the city run by the Demetros inspected for breaches of the building code . . . and while I'm at it take a fresh look at *every* unresolved money-switching complaint leveled against them in the past decade?"

"What kind of bullshit is this?" The younger guy reared suddenly from the back of his chair. "You got no goddamn right talking to my father that way."

"Janos." Demetro said with a pacifying wave of his hand. "Take it easy. . . ."

Janos shook his head furiously. "Pop, these cops got balls walking in here—"

"Enough!" Demetro roared.

He waited a moment for Janos to subside, then pulled the cigar out of his mouth and tipped it toward Pembleton like a blackboard pointer.

"I heard about those two killed at Bash's *ofisa,*" he said. "But it has nothing to do with me."

"Mihial Bash believes otherwise," Pembleton said.

"Mihial Bash is a lying cocksucker with a mouth that's bigger than his brain," Demetro said.

"Then you deny having threatened him."

Demetro took a deep pull of his cigar.

"That what he told you? I *threatened* him?"

Pembleton nodded.

"Now let *me* tell you something," Demetro said, exhaling more smoke. "Once upon a time we had a common sort of business disagreement, which I will not go into 'cause it ain't important. Mihial said a few unfriendly things to me, I said some to him. Just words. Gypsies get a little wild with the yelling and cursing. But we don't go around gunning each other down."

"How about burning each other out?" Pembleton said.

"Huh?"

"There was a fire in Mihial Bash's *ofisa* last night."

Demetro grunted and readjusted himself on the couch, his shaggy eyebrows arching. On the chair beside him Janos was touching his hair a lot as he struggled to contain his anger. Pembleton figured it was a nervous tic.

"He blame this fire on me too?" Demetro said finally.

Pembleton shook his head. "Claims he started it himself, but I don't believe him. Neither does the arson squad."

"And you think *I'm* the one plays with matches?"

"I think somebody put a Molotov cocktail through Bash's window last night, and whoever did it thought he'd be getting a free throw," Pembleton said. "This isn't going to happen."

Janos nearly jumped off his chair in sudden meltdown.

"How much of this we gotta sit here and take? You got no fucking right to accuse us of *shit*."

"Janos, I told you to calm down," Demetro said wearily, putting a hand on his son's arm.

Now Janos actually did spring to his feet.

"You wanna let these assholes walk all over you, go ahead," he snapped. "I'm getting out of here."

"Aren't you interested in seeing which contestant wins the Winnebego?" Munch said, and indicated the game show on the television set.

Janos stood there glaring at Munch a second, his mouth a slash of unbridled rage, his hands balling into fists that trembled at his sides. Then he elbowed past the detectives and stalked off toward the door.

Without looking back, Munch heard it slam open and shut.

"Maybe he'd sit still for WWF wrestling," he said to Demetro. "Or better yet the Pole Dancing Finals, if you've got pay-per-view."

Demetro's eyes shifted from Munch to Pembleton, then back to Munch again.

"Kid has a hot temper, but his heart's in the right

114

place," he said. "Cop or no cop, I won't let nobody make a joke outta him."

"Mr. Demetro, listen carefully," Pembleton said. "We don't want trouble with you or your son. But our department is conducting a homicide investigation, and it isn't going to stop. If it winds up you're holding back knowledge of the murders, there will be a *river* of trouble flowing this way, and I promise it will wash your nice little setup here right down the sewer."

Demetro puffed on his cigar. "I don't know nothing about any killings. I don't know nothing about any fire. We done now?"

Pembleton shrugged.

"If that means you are, then maybe you better leave," Demetro said. "I'm a busy man."

"We could see that when we came in," Munch said.

A moment later the two detectives turned and walked toward the door. As they were passing the bar, Bucharest triple-jumped his pal's checker pieces, then swiveled around on his bar stool and flashed his gold-toothed smile at the cops as if expecting them to be awed by his gamemanship.

"King me," he demanded triumphantly.

"These guys sure know how to live," Munch said to Pembleton.

They went out to their car.

EIGHT

"ALL RIGHT, LET'S see what we've got so far,"
Pembleton said to Munch.

They were eating lunch at the Green Pavilion, a
decent Berry Street coffee shop with skylights and
hanging plants and leaf-green booths, the bright
garden motif almost making them feel as if they
were on a picnic from the morass of suspicion and
hostility surrounding their case.

Munch took a bite of his turkey club. "How do
you like the food in this place?"

Pembleton shrugged indifferently. He was having
a cheeseburger deluxe and thought it was as good as
any.

"Ahh, I should've known," Munch said. "It's all
over your face."

Pembleton wiped his mouth with his napkin and
then inspected it for ketchup stains.

"*What's* all over my face?" he said, seeing the
napkin was clean.

"Look, Frank, there's no reason to be mad just because I asked to sit in the nonsmoking section."

Pembleton gave him a befuddled look. "Mad?"

"Well, irritated. *Peeved.* Whichever word you prefer."

"I didn't know I was either," Pembleton replied truthfully, swallowing his food. "In fact I thought we were about to compare notes—"

"In a minute. First we should get some things out in the open."

"Okay," Pembleton said. "Like what?"

"Like, for starters, your *unhappiness,* shall we say, about the booth I picked out," Munch said.

"Munch, I think it's fine—"

"But you'd prefer to be in the smoking section, right?"

Pembleton sighed. "The waitress asked both of us where we wanted to sit. Since you'd been here before and I hadn't, I *deferred* to you. If it'd mattered, I would have said something."

"Frank, you still haven't answered my question," Munch said. "Where would *you* rather be sitting?"

Pembleton wondered if the conversation they were having was somehow related to the hard time he'd given Munch the other morning, when he'd been asking around about a Gypsy restaurant.

"I'd have chosen smoking," he said.

"And why's that?"

"Because I'm a smoker. And because I like having a cigarette with my coffee after I've finished eating."

"Even though you're trying to quit smoking?"

"I'm trying to *cut back,*" Pembleton corrected.

"Frank, it's cold turkey or nothing."

Pembleton picked up his soda and rattled the ice in the glass.

"That," he said, "is your opinion."

"An educated opinion, being that I'm a former three-pack-a-day man."

Pembleton shrugged again. Five minutes ago he hadn't been mad, or peeved, or however the hell else Munch had characterized his mood—but he was slowly getting there. Why the reformed addict spiel at this juncture, when the Bash investigation gave them more than enough to talk about?

"The reason weaning yourself off cigarettes doesn't work," Munch was elaborating, "is that a habit is, by definition, impulsive. And it's your regular patterns of behavior that *trigger* these impulses."

"Meaning?"

"Break the patterns, break the habit," Munch said.

"So you had us put in nonsmoking for *my* benefit?"

"Knowing you'd reach for a butt soon as the coffee came," Munch said.

"Now I'm annoyed," Pembleton said.

"I *knew* it," Munch said.

Pembleton rubbed his temples. "We going to discuss the case or not?"

"Soon as you promise that you'll give my method of quitting a shot," Munch said.

"I told you—"

"I know, you're just cutting back," Munch said. "Which is impossible, because for every trigger you're aware of, there are a hundred you aren't, and they'll get you lighting up every time."

"Look, that's your theory," Pembleton said. "Bayliss used a nicotine patch when he quit smoking, and he *swears* by it—"

"You ask me, that was just a crutch."

"The point is, it did the trick for him."

"Wrong," Munch said. "That's *not* the point. You have to go along with this, Frank."

"With *what*?"

"Trying cold turkey so we can be better partners."

Pembleton wondered if he'd missed something.

"This conversation's making me dizzy," he said.

"Anyway, I tried quitting once. Went without a smoke for three months—"

"That was before you became a father. And before you and me."

"You and me?"

Munch crunched into a pickle and then sat there looking chagrined.

"There has to be some trust between us if we're gonna work together," he said.

Pembleton stared at him.

"I trust you plenty," he said.

"If this were a poker game, I'd know you had a pair of deuces," Munch said. "Frank, I'm talking the kind of trust that *bonds* people. That makes teams like Batman and Robin. Or you and Bayliss. Or me and Bolander."

Ah-ha, Pembleton thought. Stanley Bolander had been one of the squad's best cops, and for a long while after his departure Munch had been like a man who'd lost his arm or leg and kept feeling a phantom limb where it had been—as if Bolander's absence were only a passing phase, and their partnership a reality instead of a memory. Lately he seemed to have admitted to himself that Bolander would not be returning to active duty, but maybe that acceptance was just something he wore on the surface, something to keep people from constantly asking how he was doing and make it easier for him to get through the day.

"See, Frank," Munch was saying, "if you quit smoking altogether because I've asked you—do it my way for however long our fortunes are hitched, so to speak—then it'll be an act of faith. And we'll click as partners. It's *that* simple. Take Lennon and McCartney, for instance—"

"Never mind," Pembleton said. "I'll do it."

Munch stared at him like a kid who'd talked his parent into buying him a toy he'd thought hopelessly out of reach.

"You will?" he asked.

"Yeah," Pembleton said. "Though I'm wondering what *you* intend to do as an act of faith in *me*. Or doesn't this work both ways?"

"Sure," Munch said. "But we better save that for

later, or else we'll never get to talking about our case."

Pembleton sighed with resignation.

"You find out anything at Belvedere Court?" he said.

"Matter of fact, I did." Munch told Pembleton about Christine Bash's fortune-telling activities, and the shouting matches involving Carmen Bash and both her parents. "What gets me is how different tenants perceived the fights. I talked to a couple of them who were convinced Carmen was the daughter from hell, and blame everything on her. But on the other hand there's this woman, Gabriella Reyes, who swears she'd a good kid."

"The ones who believe Carmen was at fault," Pembleton said, "what reasons they give you?"

"Well, they're mostly senior citizens who feel she ought to wear ballroom gowns and petticoats instead of miniskirts and tights, and bow and curtsy in the presence of her elders. The one objective thread in all their comments is that she'd been truant from school."

"And Reyes?"

"Like I said, she's got an opposite take. Feels Carmen's a case for Child Welfare, in the sense that her parents would *force her* to stay home from school, then dress her up like Esmeralda in *The Hunchback of Notre Dame* and have her pass out fliers for their little magic show."

"So," Pembleton said, "Which version you buy? Is it Carmen Black or Carmen White?"

"Gabriella Reyes is the only one in the bunch who ever *talked* to the girl. And whose main connection to the world isn't Regis and Kathie Lee." Munch chewed his sandwich. "Plus there's something else. Two things, really."

Pembleton looked at him speculatively.

"According to one eyewitness, Carmen told her parents she was leaving home the night before they were aced. Said words to the effect that she had somebody who'd help her get along."

"And?" Pembleton made a winding gesture with his hand.

"Carmen told Gabriella about a cousin she looked up to, and in whom she'd confide," Munch said. "The cousin's a teacher."

"Lovera Bash," Pembleton said.

"Gotta be."

"Fits with what I got out of Mihial Bash," Pembleton said. "He confirmed, sort of, that she drives a Mustang."

"Sort of?"

"I slipped the question past his guard, asked him whether she owns a new or classic model. Of course he got defensive, said to ask *her* about it—"

"But didn't *deny* that she owns one."

Pembleton nodded, signaled for the waitress and, when she arrived, ordered two coffees.

"Okay, let's put it together," Munch said as she trotted off. "First, we have this kid at the bakery who sees Vera Bush drive past the fortune-telling joint."

"Right around the time of the murders," Pembleton added.

Munch grunted in unhappy acknowledgment.

"Second," Pembleton said, "you have several neighbors agreeing that there was friction between Carmen and her parents. Disregarding whatever spin any of them put on the relationship."

"Then there's the comment she made about taking off."

"And what she said about her cousin to the Reyes woman."

"Look, I can see where Vera might step in to help the kid with her family problems. But what exactly does that prove, except that she's a caring relative?" Munch said. "That she lures the parents to the Bash joint at six A.M. and *shoots* them? It's a lot to swallow, Frank. Especially when you add the bruises on Alexei Bash."

"How so?"

"Come *on,* Frank. You know as well as I do that Alexei got into a nasty rough-and-tumble with the shooter before he kicked. He outweighed Vera by a hundred pounds. It wouldn't have been a fight."

"She could have had somebody else do the actual hit," Pembleton said. "Waited outside, or inside, or wherever until it was over."

"*Still* doesn't jibe with the evidence. Why would her hired gun have to jimmy his way into the *ofisa* when she could have just opened the door for him? And what about the missing safe?"

"Mihial Bash denies there was one," Pembleton said.

"Mihial Bash would deny his own *existence* to us if he could," Munch said. "You and I *both* saw the cut bolts and metal shavings on the floor."

They were quiet a moment. The waitress came over and set their coffees on the table.

"Cream and sugar?" she said.

"For me," Munch said.

She reached into her apron pocket for a handful of plastic half-and-half containers, reached into it a second time for some packets of sugar, deposited them on the table and rushed off.

"Listen," Pembleton said, raising his cup to his lips. "There's still no explanation for what Lovera Bash was doing in her car, driving past the murder scene right about when the crime occurred, and she *claims* to have been home in Washington. . . ."

"Granted, she's covering up. But has it occurred to you that maybe it's to protect the kid?"

Pembleton shrugged. "Looks to me like she's involved either way."

Munch emptied a packet of sugar into his coffee, stirred it and sipped.

"You make your date with the beautiful Gypsy maiden yet?" Pembleton asked.

"Uh-uh," Munch said. "She told me the best way to get in touch was to leave a message on her machine in Washington, and that she'd be checking it remotely while she was staying in town. I called this morning before we left HQ."

"If she doesn't get back to you quick, we'd better pay her a visit."

Munch sat very still a moment and then nodded.

Pembleton drank from his cup, then wiped his mouth with his hand.

"About that date," he said. "You figure out where you're going to eat?" he asked.

"Haven't had much of a chance," Munch said.

Pembleton rubbed his chin.

"I know a good Japanese place," he said.

Munch looked at him. "Yeah?"

"Mary thinks it's romantic," Pembleton said. "You want the number for reservations?"

Munch smiled a little, still looking at him over the rim of his cup.

"Sure, partner," he said.

NINE

THE CONDO WAS on the twenty-third floor of a gleaming new Federal Hill high-rise, its glass-doored terrace offering a glorious view of the harbor, its rooms done up in subdued shades of gray and white, even the fireplace surrounded by gray marble tiles, no mantel or hearth, very sleek. Depending on which way she looked at it, the abstract metal sculpture above the fireplace resembled a Chinese fan, an oversized Roman gladiator helmet, an undersized grand piano or an alien life form winging through the atmosphere of Jupiter. Last night, when she'd had a fire going, the glow had made it seem iridescent.

David Lehman, who was both the owner of the place and benevolent lord of the anthropology department at school, had told Vera she could stay there while she was in Baltimore, a generous offer she'd been pleased to accept, knowing she would not feel comfortable in her father's home. She had expected David's place to be very much like the man himself—polished, lots of class, scrupulously immaculate—but had not envisioned this soft yet enfolding luxury that made her feel as if she had checked into a hideaway for the rich and famous rather than the occasional residence of a university scholar. Live and learn.

She came in the door now, Carmen following behind her, both of them with their long black hair twisted into braids, both moving with the long-legged grace of gazelles despite being bundled against the cold and weighted down with grocery bags, third cousins who looked so much alike they could have been mistaken for sisters. Over the past few months, Vera had frequently mused about their striking physical resemblance, and the even more remarkable similarities in their personalities, wondering whether one had overly influenced the other, only to conclude it was like the question of the chicken or the egg; who knows, what's the difference, they were two of a kind, that was all there was to it.

They swung into the kitchen, dumped their groceries on the cooking island and took off their coats, tossing them over one of the high-backed cottage chairs around the breakfast table.

"I'll do the unpacking," Carmen said.

Vera nodded. "Leave the fruit and orange juice out on the butcher block. I'm going to whip up a couple of health shakes."

Carmen reached into a bag, pulled out three

wedges of imported cheese, a container of black olives and packages of prosciutto, fresh-ground coffee and sun-dried tomatoes, filling her arms with these and a host of other items they'd carried from the speciality shop on Fawn Street, then turning to load them into the refrigerator and kitchen cabinets.

Vera watched her for a second or two before getting down to her own task. They'd been food shopping all morning, hitting Little Italy, then cabbing over to the old indoor market on Broadway, going up and down the crowded aisles, picking out fresh produce, splurging on oysters and crabmeat, Vera insisting that her niece not even *think* about price, money's no object, buy whatever does it to your taste buds. Watching Carmen at the stalls, seeing the deliberate care with which she made her selections, there had been times when it was almost possible to forget that she'd been orphaned not forty-eight hours before, that the bloodied corpses of her parents were still lying in the morgue. In that way too she reminded Vera of herself: getting things done, keeping occupied, trying to push each moment up against the next and keep a step ahead of the pain.

Vera turned and laid out her fruit on the butcher block—a peach, a banana, some strawberries, a couple of apples—then got a paring knife from a drawer and began peeling and coring. She'd planned the shopping trip partly as a diversion for her niece, but there also had been a real need to get food in the house and, very urgently, into Carmen's stomach.

She had been propelled through the traumatic events of the past few days on little but nervous energy and it was beginning to show. For a girl who probably peaked the scale at a hundred and ten pounds, there wouldn't be a lot of breathing room between the first signs of exhaustion and serious physical problems—and here again, Vera drew her understanding from personal experience. But if her own learning had been difficult, and bound up with a heavy emotional freight, how did it compare to Carmen's? To what she was going through now, and would have to cope with for the rest of her life?

". . . can hardly believe how much *stuff* you bought."

Carmen was unpacking a second bag, this one from the market. She hoisted out a large tub of ice cream, a six-pack of Coke, a jar of salsa, king-sized bags of potato and tortilla chips.

"How're we gonna eat it all?" she said.

Vera mustered a smile. "With wicked relish."

They stood there behind the counter, shoulders almost touching, looking at each other in a moment of unspoken connection. Like sisters, Vera thought again. At fourteen Carmen was tall for her age, about five-six, a dark, high-cheekboned beauty who'd be knocking men off their feet in another few years.

"You've been so great," Carmen said, her eyes suddenly moist. "I can't believe everything you're doing for me. . . ."

"Hey, we're family, aren't we?" Vera said.

"Yeah," Carmen said. "Not just any family, but Rom. And in my case, not just any Rom, but *marhime*."

Vera's face became deeply serious. That word, that awful word, it was impossible to measure how much she hated it. *Marhime*. Tainted, outcast, contaminated—definitions edged with connotations of sexual promiscuity, and rooted in the Gypsy conception that women were inherently unclean. No, she could not begin to describe her hatred for it, or count the times her parents had used it to condemn her, to overthrow her self-confidence, to imprint her with their hatreds and prejudices . . . and eventually to wash their hands of her in good conscience. If she was *marhime,* then she could be isolated from the family circle, and their standing in society would not be diminished by her refusal to conform.

Dear God, Vera thought, so her niece had been subjected that sort of mental cruelty too. It was one thing she wished they didn't have in common. And though her sorrow over what happened to Carmen's parents was honest and real, it did not entirely negate her resentment toward anyone that could lay such a damaging mark upon their own child.

"Don't ever call yourself that, Carmen," she said soberly. "Not even kidding around. It takes too much away from you."

Carmen turned away and put her latest batch of groceries in the cabinet, then stood with her back to Vera, gazing out the kitchen window, dabbing at her eyes.

Vera dropped the apple slices she was holding into the blender wiped her hands with a dishtowel, went over to her niece and gently patted her shoulder. For a moment they were both silent, looking out the window together, lemon-yellow sunlight washing over them. A magic carpet of snow had fallen over the ledges and rooftops below, blunting their hard edges, transforming the view of the city into a scene out of a winter fable. On the far horizon, Vera saw a boat crawl across the glazed surface of the harbor like a snail across a pane of glass.

"When you were first . . . on your own," Carmen said without turning toward Vera, "were you scared?"

Vera thought about the string of lousy, subservient jobs she'd endured to make her rent and college tuition, the endless come-ons and put-downs, the sense of exclusion from her family that had torn at her confidence even while she'd been learning how to survive . . . and also thought about her absolute refusal to submit to those pressures, and return to the insular world of her upbringing.

"There was that," she said, her grip on Carmen's shoulder firming. "And I was lonely a lot of the time. But mostly I knew I'd make it."

She felt a little sob shudder through Carmen's body, saw her tear-streaked face reflected in the windowpane, faint and nearly transparent.

"I really messed you up, didn't I?" Carmen said, crying openly now. "You shouldn't even be here."

"Carmen, listen—"

"The whole thing with my parents, asking you to help . . ." Carmen wiped her eyes again. "You've got your own life, your work at school. . . . How're you supposed to take care of me?"

"We'll take care of each other," Vera said, tasting salt on her lips. "I believe that would be fair enough."

They both stood quietly in the bright sunlight by the window, gazing past the flowing whiteness of the rooftops to the finger piers reaching out over the water, on whose surface the boat Vera had been watching was now just a dot against the greater Chesapeake.

"It's not your fault," Vera said after a while. "None of it."

Carmen nodded, then brought her own hand up to her shoulder and let it rest lightly on top of Vera's.

"You and me," she said.

"Yes," Vera replied. "You and me."

SOON IT WOULD all be over, Mihial Bash thought.

The revolver was a Smith & Wesson .38 Special snubnose, five-round cylinder, nice and compact, not fancy or complicated. A piece designed to be fired at close range, where a man's face could be recognized as he squeezed the trigger, and the hatred in his eyes could be seen over the flash of the barrel.

It was a gun that said what it had to say and nothing more.

Mihial sat on the edge of his bed under the chipped and flaking ceiling, his hands on his lap, the gun in his hands, looking down at it, turning it, sliding his fingers over its smooth blued barrel. He had bought it on the street, gone to this dealer he'd heard about through the grapevine, black guy called Trank who'd sold it to him right out of his flame-red Jeep, standing there in the open on North Avenue, a scarf with the Japanese rising sun emblem wrapped around his head, small diamond glinting in his right nostril, cartridge belt slung diagonally across his chest. Making a spectacle of himself, as if daring the cops or anybody else to fuck with him.

It had been maybe twelve, one o'clock, middle of the day, and he hadn't given a shit who was around, was just waiting at the curb, leaning against the side of his Jeep, passing a glass crack pipe to a woman in the front passenger seat. When Mihial arrived for the buy, he'd gone around back and hauled down the tailgate and displayed a fucking *sackful* of hardware, everything from Uzis to semiautomatics to homemade zip guns, grinning like a bandit, the tails of the Japanese rag flapping against his neck.

"You out to cap somebody?" Trank asked him with his sick, sly grin, knowing he wouldn't get an answer, just wanting to hear himself talk. "Got some mighty iron in the Jeep, name-brand goods, come to a life-or-death scene, it's like, you don't want no cheap knockoff blowin to pieces in your hand."

Mihial looked at him. "You think it's a good idea to do this out here?" he asked edgily.

The wind was kicking up, raising the stench of a trash fire in one of the alleys that snaked between the blighted row houses lining the street. Mihial looked toward the spiraling black smoke and saw a group of derelicts clustered around a blazing garbage can, wrapped in infinite layers of clothing, their faces scabbed and frostbitten.

"Ain't no button-down blues in this neighborhood," Trank laughed after a pause. "Ain't nobody here 'cept me, you, my woman and the livin dead . . . an' the heat I pack is the only thing can keep them from eatin' us alive."

Trank produced a gun from his canvas bag and held it up with the reverence of a priest handling holy sacraments. It was black, sleek and deadly looking, like a poisonous snake.

"You gonna dig the Glock, sidearm I got in my hand right now," Trank said. "Glock Model 20, ten mil auto. Kraut gun, so you know it gonna be efficient. Double-action, made a space-age plastic, light as a baby angel. Hold fifteen rounds in the magazine. Only thirty-three working parts, an' that include the clip. Real showpiece, an' a virgin— never been used before."

Mihial shook his head and told the gun dealer that he wasn't some government spy, he wanted something simple. Wanted it quick so he could get the fuck out of that stinking shithole of a neighborhood.

135

Sitting on his bed now, reaching over to his nightstand for a box of pistol cartridges, Mihial could remember Trank's disappointment as he leaned into the cargo section of his Jeep and returned the Glock to the duffel. Waiting behind him uneasily, Mihial had heard the sound of breaking glass from somewhere down the block, then a woman shrieking, then a man shouting over her screams, his voice bouncing between the crumbled, grafitti-scarred row houses in loud angry echoes. . . .

"Is this enough? Is *this* enough? *Is this enough?*"

After what seemed like a lifetime Trank showed Mihial the .38 Special, saw the sharp interest in his face and held it out for him to take.

Mihial examined the weapon carefully and decided he liked its solid weight, liked the way it felt in his hand.

And then Trank raised his own hand and fired a shot with his thumb and forefinger.

"Be all right, huh?" he said, and Mihial would never forget the way his crazyass grin grew until it seemed as if there was nothing to him *except* that grin—no eyes, no nose, no body, just those lips peeling back over his teeth.

Pushing the image from his mind, Mihial opened the ammo box, released the cylinder of the gun and began feeding rounds into it. For some reason he didn't understand, his hands were shaking badly. Twice the slugs jumped out of his fingers and he had to pick them up off the floor. His mother had fallen asleep in the next room and his nerves seemed to vibrate in the quiet apartment.

After giving Trank the cash for the revolver—it had cost him over four hundred dollars—he had rushed to escape that war zone of a neighborhood, driving past block after block of vacant, padlocked storefronts, low-income housing projects, methadone clinics and rat-infested junkyards, jolting his car over thick chunks of mixed snow and ice that had blown across the road. Once home, he'd put the gun in the nightstand and gone into the shower, stood under the steaming water as if his contact with the gun dealer had left him covered with filth.

And here he was an hour later, here he was, popping one slug after another into his gun, trembling like a man with palsy, his desire for revenge a cauldron in which all rational thought had melted away. It was as if there were nothing inside him but fire and smoke.

Mihial had never hated a man enough to want to kill him. Yet now he felt as if his pent-up fury would tear him apart unless discharged with the pulling of a trigger, the rhythmic thunder of a gun going off in his hand.

He slid a seventh round under the hammer of the revolver, then slapped the loaded cylinder into the frame and gave it a clockwise spin to make sure it was functioning smoothly.

Yes, he would blow Janos Demetro away like a paper target. Do it close, so he could see the fear and pain in his eyes as the bullets ripped into him and the life quivered from his body.

He knew where to find him, knew he could handle it himself.

Soon, he thought.

Very soon. . . .

It would all be over.

"MIHIAL BASH IS a dead man," Janos Demetro said, his voice full of contempt. "The three of us, we're gonna put him the fuck away."

He was standing outside the garage, huddled in a tight semicircle with his father's bodyguards, who'd exited the clubhouse behind Pembleton and Munch, leaving their game of checkers unfinished to make sure the cops hadn't stuck around the lot.

"You sure that's how you want it?" said the one with the floppy black hat.

"That's how I want it, Nino," Janos said.

"Old man'll throw a fit, he finds out," the other bodyguard said.

"We either deal with our problems or run from them," Janos said. "I ain't running."

He spat on the pavement, watched a crumpled candy wrapper skitter across the lot in the blustery wind. It had taken Janos a while to get himself under control after storming out of the clubhouse, and he'd walked for maybe a mile in a red fury, not giving a shit where he was going, thinking about the way those bastard cops had talked to his father— insulting him, treating him without respect, as if he were nothing but a cheap punk. Janos had taken all he could, which was more than should've been expected of him. Was he supposed to sit there with his mouth clamped shut like a fool or a coward? Was that how the son of Al Demetro dealt with the *gaje*? If he didn't stand up to them, teach them to show a little respect, who would?

"Kos got a point," Nino said. "You saw your father when the bulls told him about the fire. It ain't sittin' right with him."

"Tell me about it," Janos said.

Nino shrugged. "What's he gonna say if we take this thing further?"

"And then there's Pulika," Kos said. "He finds out, he'll—"

"It don't matter what the fat man thinks." Janos's eyes darkened in anger. "Look, you two with me or not?"

Kos opened his mouth, closed it, then glanced tensely over at Nino, as if letting him make up both their minds.

"Nobody said we weren't," Nino said. "We just want to know how to set it up."

"Let me worry about that," Janos said, still spearing them with his gaze. "All you gotta do is keep watching the girl's apartment, and be ready when I say it's time. And remember that I want Bash to see my face when I ace him."

All three looked at each other in silence. The wind roller-coastered madly and Nino pushed his

139

hat down over his brow to keep it from blowing away.

"Now, get back inside and keep the old man company," Janos said. "I don't want him busting you guys."

Kos immediately turned toward the garage, but Nino hesitated a moment, regarding Janos in the lashing gusts.

"What is it?" Janos said.

"You really hate Bash that much," he said.

Janos's lips twisted into a vicious parody of a grin.

"Only while he's still living," he said.

TEN

FAT LOUIE PULIKA was voluminous in both body and temperament, a grand three-ring circus of a man, a man whose bacchanalian feast of experience made the sum total of most people's lives seem like nursing home coffee klatches . . . or so he chose to have them believe. Fat Louie would never *enter* a room so much as *impose* himself upon it, or *converse* so much as *issue proclamations,* or *eat* his meals so much as *revel* in them, and so on and so forth, every gaudy facet of his appearance lifting him above the pedestrian, every exaggerated mannerism broadcasting the message that he was the Big Time—make that capital B, capital T, chum.

When Pembleton and Munch arrived at his Charles Avenue *ofisa* for their witching hour audience, they were led by an underling into the back room, where they found Fat Louie seated high above them in an ornate black gypsy wagon, pomaded and mustachioed, his vast upper bulk regally draped in a tassled gold vest and flowing purple shirt of brocaded satin, his waist swathed in a wide purple sash, his feet coddled by gleaming black leather cossack boots, and his ringed and braceleted hands festooned with enough eyecatchingly precious gems to fill a display case at Harry Winston's. The walls around him were a gallery of exotic Oriental hangings, and dramatic silver and enamel handicrafts imported from far and wide. The pattern rugs beneath his wagon wheels were lush and leagues deep. A riotous collection of embroidered cushions had been flung about the room in lieu of conventional chairs.

"Right on time, boys!" Fat Louie trumpeted, glancing down at a gold pocket watch in his palm. He tucked the watch into his vest and gestured toward a pair of cushions. "The rug's an antique, so take your shoes off and sit, why don't you?"

The cops looked at each other and then did as he'd asked, feeling as if they'd entered a scene from *Arabian Nights*—or maybe *The King and I*—as they pulled up a couple of pillows.

"How about some cognac to take the rattle outta your bones?" Fat Louie said, clapping his hands with such enthusiasm a cymbal on the wall bonged in sympathy.

"Thanks," Munch said, "but we're on duty."

"I got Courvasier and you're gonna be *formal*?"

"Mr. Pulika, we're very appreciative of your time and hospitality—" Pembleton began.

Fat Louie thrust his hand out in a halting gesture.

"Hey, you want me to be straight, I hate coppers," he said. "But Harry Grogan vouches that you're okay, and for him I make exceptions."

Pembleton wondered whether he'd just been praised or insulted.

Fat Louie's hand reached down into the wagon and surfaced a moment later with a box of wrapped chocolates. Neither detective was surprised to see the Godiva imprint on the lid.

"Who's Munch?" Fat Louie inquired, peeling the foil off a chocolate nugget and sticking it in his mouth.

"Over here," Munch said.

"Harry says you're the guy I should talk to."

"I suppose," Munch said, at a loss.

"So what do you want from me?" Pulika clapped his hands like Yul Brynner again.

"As you probably know," Munch said, "my partner and I are looking into a murder—"

"Nobody gives a damn when Gypsies get killed," Pulika said.

"Well, if that were true, we wouldn't be here right now," Munch said.

"Yeah, right." Pulika tweaked the left-hand curl of his mustache. "You guys gotta put on a show."

"Being that it's midnight," Pembleton said, "and we're here alone, who do you think we're putting on a show for?"

"I wasn't talking to you," Pulika said. "But since the question's been raised, let me clarify that I didn't mean this *visit,* I meant your investigation in general. You ain't nothing but whitewashers."

Pembleton frowned. "With all due respect, sir—"

"Look, it's no problem, I accept it as a sad fact of life," Pulika interrupted. "Nobody gives a damn if Gypsies live or die, if they get robbed, beaten or raped, if they starve in the fucking gutters. To you *gaje* we're all a bunch of lazy, cheating thieves, and racial inferiors to boot. Which is why we take care of our own."

"The way somebody took care of Alexei and Christine Bash?" Pembleton asked, tiring of Pulika's recitation.

The wagon's undercarriage creaked and groaned as Pulika heaved his poundage forward.

"They weren't killed by Rom!" he boomed crossly.

"How can you be positive?" Munch said. "We know that Mihial Bash himself is convinced the Demetro clan's responsible—"

"Mihial has a brain like a frog, poke him and he jumps," Pulika said. "He doesn't know what the hell he's talking about."

"Why would he point the finger at someone without any reason?"

"I didn't say he didn't have his reasons," Pulika replied. "I said he was wrong."

"We were hoping you could help us understand his animosity toward the Demetros," Pembleton said.

Pulika stared at him. "What's your name, buddy?"

"Frank Pembleton."

"Well, Frank, you ought to learn some patience," Pulika said with a double hand clap.

Pembleton said nothing. He didn't exactly get what the hand clapping routine was about but it was starting to give him a headache.

"This thing between the Demetros and Bashes goes back maybe twenty, thirty years," Pulika said. "Before either family got to Baltimore."

Munch looked at him, confused. "Grogan said it was about turf."

"He's right," Pulika said, clearly milking the moment. "And he's wrong."

"I'm listening," Munch said.

"Used to be the Bashes, the Demetros and four, five other families were all in the same *kumpania*," Pulika said. "Made camp down in Georgia and the Carolinas—this is when a lot of us still slept in tents, traveled around with road shows and county fairs."

"Telling fortunes?" Munch asked.

"That was for the women," Pulika said. "The men hired out to the carnies as hands and gofers, and the ones with some kind of talent got jobs with the show. They were musicians, jugglers, fire-eaters, animal trainers . . . and fancy horseback riders, which is where the trouble got started."

"This is about *horses?*"

"It's about what happens when a married guy lets some local working girl ride *his* saddle," Pulika said. "The horse was an innocent bystander."

"You're losing me," Munch said.

Pulika's cryptic, amused smile made it clear that had been precisely his intention.

"Mihial Bash, he was maybe twenty years old at the time. His wife had just had a baby girl—"

"Vera?" Munch said, figuring she fit the bill agewise.

"Yeah," Pulika said. "Was a rough birth, small fry came out feet first, almost choked on her umbilical cord. Tore the mother up pretty bad. Mihial had to do without for a long time afterward . . . or should have been doing without, you catch my meaning."

"He get something going on the side while his wife was recovering?" Munch said.

"What he mostly had going was booze," Pulika said. "But pour enough firewater in his tank and the guy'd spin out of control. One night he gets his horns up, picks up some scab who was hanging around the midway, brings her back to camp . . . Don't ask me why he didn't go to her place, or some fucking motel." Pulika released a huge sigh. "Since, for obvious reasons, he can't very well bring this woman back to his tent, and doesn't want to be seen by his wife's relatives, he bops her under the starry sky in the clearing where the families hitched their horses."

"That's taking the expression 'a roll in the hay' too literally, you ask me," Munch said. "Unless pony poop's some kind of funky aphrodisiac."

Fat Louie dissolved into laughter, his head bobbing, the meaty folds under his chin shaking and jiggling, his belly heaving up and down in uproarious swells of flesh. His wagon rocked and swayed.

"Grogan told me you were a hoot," he said, wiping tears from his eyes.

Munch glanced at Pembleton and shrugged. Behind them one of the *baro*'s flunkies poked his head into the doorway and quickly withdrew it, probably curious about his boss's eruption of mirth.

"Getting back to Mihial," Fat Louie said after a while, "I dunno whether he rolled over any horse pucky that night, but he *did* roll over the rope Al Demetro used to tie his favorite stallion to a tree. See, he'd used a long piece so the beast would be able to roam around if he wanted, and there was plenty of slack on the ground. Imagine Mihial and the broad goin' at it, gettin' the horses all nervous and skittish, tumbling back and forth over the part of the rope that's laying in the grass, when who should pop his head into the clearing but Demetro himself, checking to see what's keeping his animal up past its bedtime."

Fat Louie shook with another burst of laughter.

"You just lost me again," Munch said blankly. "I'm sure Mihial in the buff is a sorry spectacle, but I don't see the problem for Demetro."

"That's because you don't know what it is to be *marhime*," Fat Louie said.

"Think you could explain?"

"Let's just say that we Gypsies got our moral code—which I'm sure will surprise you two—and that adultery is one of the things that's frowned upon, and that there are strict punishments for anybody who's caught stepping out on the spouse. Let's also say that, according to tribal law, anything that physically comes in contact with someone who's *committing* adultery is considered to be defiled. You starting to get the picture?"

The two cops sat there a moment, Fat Louie's question hanging in front of them.

"Bash defiled Demetro's horse?" Pembleton said finally.

"By extension," Fat Louie said, nodding. "Since his sweaty flesh really just touched the rope."

Munch was scratching his head.

"Weird," he muttered.

"Maybe to your average *gajo*," Fat Louie said. The amusement had abruptly left his features. "As a cop, though, you ought to have a better perspective. I mean, why does *anybody* have laws? We Rom were nomads for centuries. Enough of us still are. You move from place to place, things tend to get confusing unless there's strict rules. Ones you better not break. Ones that don't change no matter where you go. The idea of *marhime*'s a way of keeping order."

"As far as these rules went for Demetro's horse," Pembleton said, "are you saying it had to be destroyed?"

"Now you're catching on," Fat Louie said. "Al was heartbroken, not to mention crazy mad, and he made a formal complaint to the tribal judges, demanding some kind of compensation from Bash.

Next, the judges went ahead and held a council. Hit Mihial with heavy damages, besides laying public shame on him for stepping out on his poor wife."

"Naturally Mihial was thrilled to pay up," Pembleton said.

"Oh yeah, right." Fat Louie shook his head. "First he tried to make like Al was lying about what he saw. When that didn't fly with the judges—who couldn't see why Demetro would have his prize piece of horse meat put down just for the chance to bad-mouth a kinsman—Mihial insisted that touching the horse's *rope* while fucking out of wedlock wasn't the same thing as touching the *horse,* in which case *only* the rope was *marhime.* And when five out of six judges told him where to shove that argument, the stubborn bastard claimed he didn't have the cash to pay Demetro. Which may or may not have been bullshit."

"And then . . . ?" Munch prompted.

"Then the judges told Mihial that if he was really so broke, he could square things with Demetro by giving him his daughter."

"You're kidding," Munch said, incredulous. "Wasn't that kind of *drastic*?"

"Like I already said, you should try looking at it from our point of view," Fat Louie answered, and popped another chocolate into his mouth. "That circus horse of Demetro's was a big source of income to his family. By the same token, we put a high value on women because they're readers and dependable moneymakers. When you figure that Lovera Bash was going to grow up in a tainted household if she stayed put, and that the Demetros were respected members of the *kumpania* who'd swear to raise her like one of their own, maybe the judges don't seem so extreme."

"How'd things turn out?" Pembleton asked, hurrying Pulika along. Not only did his head hurt, but he was getting a sore back and legs from squatting cross-legged on the cushion. Also Olivia would be up for a feeding in an hour or so, and he wanted to be home in time to help with it.

"Mihial slipped off with the wife and kid, didn't tell anybody where he was heading," Fat Louie said.

"And that's when he came to Baltimore," Pembleton said.

"Yeah."

"And Demetro?"

"Took years before he found out where Mihial was," said Fat Louie. "I don't know whether Al was tipped off or what, but he and his clan finally got after Bash and called him on his debt."

"And Mihial politely declined to settle," Munch said.

"By this time the fucking unreasonable jackass has his *ofisa* and is doing okay. Since the word is that his daughter's got problems, Al doesn't ask for her, even though she's maybe thirteen years old and ripe for bringing in the bucks. Bash could've paid out of pocket and been done with it clean and easy, or given Al a skim off his earnings—whichever. Instead he sends Demetro walking."

"We're hemorrhaging bad blood," Munch said.

Fat Louie spread his hands philosophically. "While Al's in town trying to collect, he decides he likes city life, gets his own businesses going, makes out well for himself. Pretty soon he's doing better than Mihial and kind of lets him slide for what he owes. Things stayed quiet between them for years."

"What made the feud heat up lately?" Pembleton asked.

"Not what," Fat Louie said. "*Who.*"

Pembleton looked at him.

"Janos," he said.

Fat Louie nodded and adjusted himself in his chariot. "I'm only talking to you as a favor to Harry Grogan. Anything you find out tonight, you didn't get from me."

The cops waited.

"Janos thinks he's an operator, but he's nothing but a spoiled punk with dumb ideas," Fat Louie said. "About six months back he comes to see me, says he wants me to call another council having to do with Bash's debt to his father, turn over all the old dirt after twenty fucking years. Seems Al's been letting the kid take care of bigger and bigger chunks of the family business, and Janos got in his head to collect what Mihial owes. Plus interest, which he called 'sanctions.' Wanted me to give Bash an ultimatum: pay up or turn over his *ofisa* to the Demetros."

"What'd you do?" Munch asked.

"I told him to take a walk," Pulika said. "There's maybe a thousand Rom in Baltimore, tops, and we got to stick together. I don't want nobody stirring up trouble."

"The kid start kicking and screaming?" Munch said.

Fat Louie chuckled. "Guess you've met him."

"Yeah."

"Janos got no self-control. He blew a fit right here in front of me, said he'd get what he wanted out of Bash, and get it his way."

Silence.

Finally Pembleton said, "You told us before that Gypsies weren't responsible for the murders of Alexei and Christine Bash. Now you seem to be saying something else."

Fat Louie shook his head.

"Janos didn't kill anybody," he said. "He had no reason."

"We think a safe was removed from Bash's *ofisa* at the time of the shootings," Pembleton said. "Janos could've broken into the place believing nobody would be around, gotten surprised by Alexei and Christine—"

"I just said he had no reason!" Fat Louie blared with an emphatic hand clap that got the cymbals on the wall resonating again.

"Mr. Pulika, I'd rather not be here all night," Pembleton persisted. He'd had his fill of the *baro*'s showboating. "If you can explain *why* you're convinced Janos is innocent, please do so."

Fat Louie scowled at Pembleton, and for a moment looked as if he would imperiously cast them from his presence. But then he got hold of himself . . . probably realizing that mixing it up with a couple of homicide cops would not be in his best interest, Pembleton thought.

At last Fat Louie released a gusty sigh, and said, "When Janos started putting the strongarm on Mihial, Alexei and Christine came up with a way to pay up for him. And not with money, either."

Pembleton sat perfectly still. Munch looked at him, then looked at Fat Louie, his eyes wide with a kind of constricting shock.

Not with money.

"My God," he said. "Carmen."

"Carmen," Fat Louie said.

ELEVEN

PEMBLETON'S SECOND RULE of Detection: Never
allow the number of hours in the day to exceed the
number of cigarettes smoked in the same period.
The adverse consequences in terms of mood and
mental acuity if the rule were broken could be
severe, especially when aggravated by lack of sleep.

Having gone almost twenty-four hours without a
butt *or* sleep—the former thanks to his lamebrained
and lamented promise to Munch, and the latter due
to back-to-back late-night sessions with his daughter Olivia and Fat Louie Pulika—Pembleton felt
anything but his best, and held few expectations that
the day would be either easy or productive.

Be that as it may, the first thing Wednesday
morning—actually, the first thing after enduring
three cups of lousy squad room coffee, roll call and
G's daily reminder about black being beautiful,
especially on the Board, ha-ha—he drove over to
Waylon Avenue for another talk with Tony D'Angelo,

who remained the only witness to place Vera Bash near the *ofisa* around the time of the killings.

Despite the tangle of hostilities between the Demetros and Mihial Bash, she was developing as the closest Pembleton had to an actual suspect in the case. While he agreed with Munch that she seemed physically incapable of having overpowered Alexei Bash in a life-and-death struggle, and in that way inflicting the punishment that had left his lifeless body covered with bruises, Pembleton still saw no reason why she couldn't have had an accomplice at the scene who *was* strong enough to do the deed.

And then there was Fat Louie's tip about Carmen. If she and Vera had a close relationship—as Munch believed they did from his questioning of Gabriella Reyes, the nurse who lived in the apartment building where the Bashes had been superintendents—then it wasn't hard to see how Vera could have been drawn into an emotional confrontation with Carmen's parents. One thing Pembleton had found to be true over the years was that the family dynamic was as volatile as nitroglycerine; in fact, a disproportionately large percentage of the murders he'd investigated had turned out to have been committed by relatives of the victims. Put family members in a pressure cooker and they often did the most godawful things to each other, things they would never do to anyone else under any other circumstances.

As he walked into the bakery now, Pembleton was hoping he'd be able to jog Tony D'Angelo's recollections about what he'd seen the morning of the killings, and get him to clarify his statement about someone having been in the Mustang with Vera Bash. If D'Angelo could help identify whoever else was in the car, it would go a long way toward cracking the case, which would be oh so nice, now, wouldn't it?

"Hey, Detective!" Tony was ringing up a sale behind the counter. "Guess your wife liked our pineapple tarts."

"Loved them." Pembleton took a whiff of the aroma coming from the ovens in back. It was the warm, yeasty smell of baking bread—rye, he thought, although it might have been sourdough.

"So what can I do for you today?"

"Well, actually I'd like to follow up on a couple of things you mentioned in your statement," Pembleton said. "Shouldn't take long."

"No problem," Tony said. "I'll—"

He turned his head toward the door to the back room as it swung open and a middle-aged woman came through onto the sales floor.

"Mom, this is Detective Pembleton. Detective, my mother, Francine," he said.

The woman smiled a little uncertainly, which hardly surprised Pembleton, since the average citizen was always ambivalent when introduced to cops, who were usually either bringing or responding to bad news and trouble.

"How do you do?" Francine D'Angelo put her hand out and Pembleton took it. She was slender and attractive, with short brown hair and a face that might have looked youthful if not for the nest of lines around her eyes. "My son mentioned that an officer had been here about those Gypsies."

Them, their, those, Pembleton thought. Here we go again.

"Well, whenever there's a crime of this sort, we routinely speak to the victims' immediate neighbors," Pembleton said. "People often aren't aware how much they notice."

"You think what I told you the other day might be important?" Tony asked.

Pembleton gave him an indeterminate shrug and took out his pad. The moment witnesses were informed their recollections would have strong bearing on an investigation, they tended to begin shading them for one reason or another, making it best to keep them in the dark.

"Tony, I really want you to focus on who was in the blue Mustang," Pembleton flipped back to the notes he'd taken during their earlier conversation. "You said you were looking out the front window when it passed, is that right?"

The kid nodded.

"And that it was heading north, toward Thatcher."

The kid nodded again.

"Which means your view would have been of the driver's side."

Nod.

"And you're absolutely certain you recognized the person driving the car?"

"Like I said, it was that Gypsy's daughter—"

"Lovera," the kid's mother interjected.

"Excuse me, ma'am?"

"Lovera Bash," she said. "My son told me he saw her."

"Oh," Pembleton said, scanning his notes. "Were you acquainted with her?"

"And Christine," Francine said. "I'm sure Tony's mentioned something about it."

"Well, actually—"

"I didn't," Tony said.

Pembleton looked at him. Last time they'd spoken, the kid had not only failed to tell him that either he or his mother had personal contact with the Bashes, but strongly suggested the contrary, and stated outright that he didn't know their names.

"Why *not*?" he asked, puzzled.

"It seemed like it wasn't important," Tony said.

Pembleton kept looking at him.

"But you made a *point* of saying—"

"I think," Francine broke in again, "Tony was embarrassed."

"What do you mean?"

A glance shuttled between mother and son.

"What do you mean?" Pembleton repeated.

And waited.

"You see, I'd gone to Christine for readings," Francine said finally, still watching her son's face. "Tony didn't agree with it, and I'm sure it's not the sort of information he would've wanted to share with anyone."

"I'm not anyone," Pembleton said. "I'm the police."

"Hey, I really apologize," Tony said. "I guess I should've said something to you."

"You have to understand, this only started after Jack passed away," Francine said.

"Jack?"

"My husband," Francine said. "He had a heart attack last year. It was very sudden."

"Mom was all broken up," Tony said. "For a while I was afraid she'd get sick too."

"Our creditors couldn't wait for the funeral to be over before they started ringing the phone off the hook, which I suppose is an old story," she said. "I could hardly manage getting out of bed at the time, let alone dealing with banks and wholesalers. Losing someone you've been married to for thirty years, and then having to face the world . . . I don't know if you have any idea what it's like."

"I can only begin to imagine," Pembleton said sympathetically, and took a moment to gather his thoughts. "Mrs. D'Angelo, if you don't mind my asking . . . who initiated these readings? Was it you or Christine—"

"It was Mihial," she said. "He used to shop here once in a while. We were closed for almost a month after Jack died, and Tony'd put a sign in our window for our customers, and Mihial came in—"

"A sign?"

"So the regulars would know there'd been a death in the family, and that we weren't closed for good," Tony said. "Dad knew most of them by name. *And* what they usually bought."

"People were very kind," Francine D'Angelo added. "We must have received dozens of condolence cards."

"And Mihial?"

"Just after we reopened, he came in with Christine and introduced her to me, told me she was very good at problem solving," Francine said. "Those were the exact words he used, by the way."

"Problem solving."

"Yes," she said.

"Should have said *hustling,*" Tony said.

"Tony always disapproved," Francine said. She looked upset. "But Christine understood so much about me right off. I mean, she reached over the counter, took hold of my hand and described what I was feeling in a way that even *I* couldn't. How I knew that I had decisions to make about money and other things, and didn't know which way to turn. . . ."

She shook her head and sighed.

"Christine told me she would do everything in her power to help me with my life choices," she continued sadly.

"Such as?"

She gave him a hesitant look, then shook her head vaguely. "Different things."

"Mom wasn't the only one got suckered, either," Tony said. "Ask around, you'll see how much

161

money the Gypsies made off people in the neighborhood."

Pembleton scribbled something in his pad.

"These readings, did they take place in the storefront down the block?" he asked Francine.

"Yes."

"And how many sessions were there all together?"

She shrugged. "Several."

"Can you be more specific?"

She shook her head, looking increasingly distressed.

"Put me in the ballpark. Were there two? Three?"

"I'm just not sure."

"And how much did you pay Christine for these consultations?"

"Well, again, it's hard to say. Sometimes she didn't take *any* money."

"But when she did? Just estimate."

Her cheeks had reddened, and her hands were tightly linked in front of her baker's apron. "I—"

"Detective Pembleton, I don't see how this has anything to do with those two people getting killed," Tony said.

"I'm almost finished," he said, glancing quickly at Tony before turning back to Francine. "Ma'am, the more I can learn about the activities of the Bashes, the better my chances of getting to the bottom of—"

"Mom, we gotta get to work," Tony said, and took hold of her elbow. His friendly attitude had been replaced by something very different. "We been trying to answer all your questions, Detective. The place gets crowded around lunchtime, and unless we finish our baking there'll be nothing for the customers to buy."

"Mrs. D'Angelo—"

"My son's right," she said, a strained expression on her face. "Maybe you had better come back."

Pembleton looked alternately at Francine and the kid, then decided it would be a waste of time to keep pushing. For whatever reason, the chill had set in.

"Okay," he said at last. "I'll be in touch."

"Sure," Tony said. He had not yet released his mother's arm. "We'll be glad to talk to you."

Pembleton closed his pad and turned toward the door.

Glad?

He had the impression that nothing could have been further from the truth.

NORIKOHANA, THE JAPANESE restaurant Pembleton had recommended, was in a glossy new section of the Harborplace complex, and Munch had made dinner reservations there moments after Vera Bash hooked up with him by phone Wednesday morning. Throughout the rest of the day he'd had a hard time deciding whether to be businesslike or casual with Vera, and had finally opted to let the matter settle itself when they got together. There was no turning away from his belief that she was at the center of some of the biggest unanswered questions of his ongoing murder investigation. Nor, however, could he forget the little zing he'd felt from head to toe when she'd flashed her sparkling smile at him. Still, he figured he'd be okay as long as he kept the distinctions straight in his mind.

They'd arranged to meet around seven at the restaurant, wound up practically bumping into each other near its entrance, and were now sitting cross-legged on reed mats in the tatami room, teacups steaming on the low natural wood table between them.

Though they were still waiting for their appetizers, Munch figured he was already well on the way toward making a lousy impression.

". . . and at first I didn't see how come my partner—*temporary* partner, I mean—was so annoyed at me for trying to find a Gypsy restaurant," he was saying to his own mortification.

Not for the life of him did he understand why he'd started out the evening by bringing up his tiff with Pembleton, or why he'd stayed on the subject, trying to explain himself, then explain his explanations, then explain his explanations of his explanations, and on and on until he felt as if he'd sunk to his earlobes in conversational quicksand—and all without any prodding from his date, who'd been listening quietly, now and then responding with what Munch hoped was a tolerant smile.

"Maybe I was being defensive," he continued, as if shutting up would give his embarrassment an ever wider field in which to thrive. "Probably, that is. But it's hard to take when out of the blue somebody accuses you of being prejudiced."

She bit her lower lip, still smiling obscurely. There were little upslanted lines at the corners of her mouth that suggested she found a lot of things amusing.

"So what do you think?" he said expectantly. "Am I a biased jerk or an open-minded and considerate fellow?"

She brought her teacup to her lips and sipped from it, and then held it level with her chin, turning it in her hands, watching him steadily through faint curls of steam.

"What won't a Gypsy ever leave home without?" she said at last, her eyes twinkling as if they contained tiny chips of diamond.

He gave her a surprised and hesitant look.

"Well?" she said. "Are you biting or what?"

He shrugged. "I give up."

"Your missing American Express card," she said, her smile breaking wide open, bright and lovely as a spring morning.

Now he was grinning. "Guess that means you're voting for open-minded and considerate."

"It means you should lighten up and stop making things worse for yourself," she said.

"Well," he said, leaning forward, "What do you get when you put two Jewish guys together in one room?"

She waited for the punch line, her eyes still gleaming.

"Three opinions."

She laughed. "How many Gypsy fortune-tellers does it take to play Lotto?"

"I don't know," he said. "How many?"

"Two," she said. "One to predict who'll buy the winning ticket, the other to pick it out of his pocket."

His grin widened.

"Okay, I've got another one," he said. "What do you get when you cross a Jew with a Gypsy?"

"Shoot."

"A thief with a guilty conscience."

She laughed. "Not bad."

"Especially since I just thought it up," he said.

"Really?"

He gave her the scout's honor sign. "People may question my political correctness, but my wit's indisputable."

They sat quietly while two waitresses in delicate peach-colored kimonos arrived with a serving dish of vegetable tempura and a tray of condiments in stone dipping bowls. They carefully arranged the various items on the table and flitted away like butterflies.

"I know this must seem like an awfully trite question," she said when they'd gone, "but how'd you get interested in police work?"

Munch snared a broccoli spear with his chopsticks and looked at her. The light in the restaurant

166

was diffuse coming through the white paper of shoji lamps; it gave warm, lovely accents to her dark features.

"I've got a brother in the drywall business, close relatives that run a funeral home and other family members with even more horrible professions—"

"More horrible than an undertaker?"

"I kid you not," Munch said. "After seeing what their jobs were like, chasing killers and drug dealers seemed a pleasant alternative."

"You give that answer often?" she said, and smiled again.

"Couple times," he said.

"I didn't mean to pry," she said. "It's just that I haven't known many cops, and the few I've run across have always been kind of humorless."

"Me being the notable exception," he said.

"Yes," she said, and slipped a vegetable into her mouth.

Munch was thinking that some women even had a way of looking sexy when they ate—especially, for some reason, when they ate vegetables and other low-fat foods that could be neatly consumed. These foods, he'd long ago decided, where inherently feminine. Yin foods, as opposed to the yang of red meat on a bun. Following that logic, he sometimes wondered whether his two ex-wives might have secretly found him more appealing and manly if he'd say, insisted on an exclusive diet of steak and burgers, scarfed down his food like a Neanderthal and let out a loud, ripping belch after each meal.

"So," he said, "did you only accept my dinner invite because my un-coplike sense of humor makes me interesting from an academic point of view?"

"Not only," she said, and smiled a little.

"Then the rest of it must be that you want the lowdown on what the police are doing to find Alexei and Christine's murderers."

"Actually," she said, "I was trying to decide if you asked me out to learn more about the mysterious inner workings of the Bash family."

Munch gazed at her face a moment. Quiet conversation rippled from a nearby table to blend with the ambient murmur of the busy restaurant.

"Not only," he said.

They sat there looking at each other as the two butterflies gracefully alighted and cleared their appetizer dishes.

"Why didn't you tell me about Carmen the day of the murders?" Munch asked.

She dipped her head a little and remained quiet, her fingers meshing on the table.

Munch still had not taken his eyes off her. "If you're trying to protect her—"

"Believe me," she said, "Carmen had nothing to do with her mother and father getting shot."

"Can you tell me what happened between them and Carmen on Saturday night?" he said.

"She didn't kill anyone."

"Vera, please," Munch said. "I know about the agreement your father had reached with the Demetros, know Carmen was being turned over to them—"

She looked across at him, her eye shiny and intense. "You've been talking to people," she said.

He nodded.

"Well, they should, get their facts straight," she said brusquely. "Carmen's parents worked out that insane trade all on their own. My father didn't want any part of it."

"I thought it was done to relieve Mihial's debt," he said.

"Maybe that was the excuse Alexei and Christine needed so they could live with themselves afterward," Vera said. "But the whole thing was cooked up strictly for their own profit. Janos Demetro pays them five thousand dollars, they turn their flesh and blood over to him as if she's a slave on the block. The 'debt relief' was Janos's way of icing the deal for them."

"I don't see what he'd have to gain by connecting the two transactions."

"That's because of your cultural perspective," she said. "Besides having babies, the woman's role in a traditional Rom family is to make money, and they do that by giving readings. Husbands aren't ashamed to let their wives be the breadwinners, and they usually won't even pick up the telephone in her place of business. I couldn't *begin* to estimate the value of a pretty girl who can lure street traffic into an *ofisa* by sitting in the window and looking seductive."

"What about Carmen's parents?" Munch asked. "Bailing out Mihial must've been worthwhile to them in some way . . . or were they just generous souls?"

"Oh, sure," Vera said in a brittle tone. "Look, my mother passed away years ago. That left my father with a fortune-telling parlor and no fortune-teller. His solution was to take on partners."

Munch raised his eyebrows. "Alexei and Christine."

"Right," she said. "I don't know the exact details of this arrangement, but Christine was Dad's reader and she got a split of the take."

"And wanted to make sure Janos didn't start cutting into that split."

She nodded.

"He was putting pressure on my father to settle his account, and I think Dad was finally going to do it," she said. "He's afraid of Janos."

He regarded her without speaking. They had ordered shabu-shabu as a dinner for two and now the waitress came with an iron kettle and a tabletop burner, set them up on the table and filled the kettle with broth from a stone terrine. They briefly glided off again, and returned with little trays of uncooked shrimp and artfully sliced beef and vegetables, as well as little wire baskets with bamboo handles for immersing the food in the heated broth.

"This is a lot to eat," he said.

"Yes."

"You very hungry after what we've been discussing?"

"No."

"Me neither," he said. "How about we have a food fight?"

She smiled faintly.

"There's something else I need to ask you," he said. "The morning your cousins were killed . . . you told me you were in D.C., and that your father called to let you know what had happened about eight o'clock. That you didn't get to Baltimore until—"

"I remember what I told you," she said.

"We have a witness who claims he saw you driving away from the *ofisa* before daybreak," he said.

He waited for her to reply but she said nothing. She was closing up, her eyes losing their luminous quality, becoming flat and remote.

"Look," he said. "I honestly wish we were talking about our favorite music, or whether you're a Shemp or a Curlie fan, or a thousand other things. But two people are dead and neither of us can get away from it."

She remained silent.

"I want to be on your side," he said.

"Do you?"

His gaze met hers. "Very much."

She gave him a little shrug.

"That's exactly what I said to Carmen when she phoned me Sunday night, you know," she told him.

171

"Janos Demetro was coming for her the next morning and she didn't have any intention of sticking around."

"But she was fourteen years old. With nowhere to go and nobody who really gave a damn," Munch said. "Except you."

"She confides in me," she said, nodding again. "Carmen's a lot like I was at her age. Independent, into school, wants more from life than anyone's willing to let her have, at least without a fight. She plans to go to college, and I'd promised to help in any way possible when the time came."

"And Sunday night . . ."

"She was ready to bum some cash, buy a Greyhound ticket to the farthest destination she could afford, become one of the missing. Up till that point she hadn't mentioned the horrible deal her parents had made, and I guess she felt bad about getting me involved. Just called from a pay phone to say she was going, and that she loved me and would be in touch."

She let the sentence trail off, her eyes suddenly becoming moist.

"What time was this?" Munch asked quietly.

"Maybe two, three o'clock."

"Monday morning?"

"Yes," Vera said. "She'd been roaming the streets all night after walking out on her parents. In the middle of the snowstorm."

"That's when you drove down to Baltimore, isn't it?"

She nodded. "I was worried sick. I told her I'd come pick her up, that she could live with me in Washington for as long as she wanted. She didn't want to go back to her parents' apartment, so we made plans to meet at my father's place."

"Weren't you afraid Mihial would just send her home?"

"Listen, my father's set in his beliefs, and his family values aren't anything like the ones our virtuous government representatives are always spouting off about, but he'd never think of selling a kid. He could have done that to me, you know."

"I heard about it," Munch said, and sighed. "Tell me the rest of what happened that night."

"Dad wasn't home when Carmen got there, but my grandmother was, and she let her in."

"Heard the doorbell?"

"Select tones and frequencies penetrate her deafness."

He smiled a little. "Go on."

She started to say something, hesitated, wiped at a stray tear that had overspilled her eyelid.

"Want a tissue?"

She shook her head and took a deep breath. "The roads were so bad in the snow, I couldn't drive faster than thirty-five," she said. "It must've been after six by the time I got to the *ofisa*. The first thing I noticed when I pulled up was that the lights were on and the door was wide open. Then I saw Carmen in there. She'd been upstairs. . . . She heard the gunshots and went down to check out what happened. . . ."

173

She drew in her shoulders and took another breath, trying not to cry. Munch had an idea she was very practiced at controlling her emotions; it was something that happened naturally when you grew up being different from the people around you. In Vera's case, she must have been isolated both from her family and the non-Gypsies they'd lived among.

It was all too much for her now, though. She lowered her head and sobbed, the tears rolling down her cheeks in a sudden flood, slicking her face with moisture.

Watching her, Munch felt his own throat tighten. He would have liked to put his arms around her.

This time when he offered her a Kleenex she accepted with a nod of thanks, dabbing her eyes and face.

"Carmen . . . it was Carmen that found her parents," she said, and took a ragged breath. The words were coming faster, as if crowding through an escape hatch that might slam shut at any moment. "They were lying on the floor, and there was blood everywhere. . . . When I picture it, I—I don't know how she copes."

"What about the shooter?" Munch said. "Did Carmen see him?"

She shook her head.

"Vera, if she knows anything—"

"She *doesn't*," she said insistently, looking straight at him, her eyes fierce and remarkably steady through the tears. "A gun was fired, and a lot more than once. That makes a lot of noise. You're the detective. . . .

Do you really think whoever killed Alexei and Christine was going to stick around?" '

Munch inhaled, exhaled slowly.

"Let's back up a second," he said. "I still don't think you've said what Carmen's parents were doing at the *ofisa*."

"I can only guess they were looking for her," she said. "They knew that I'd been talking to Carmen, and that my father disapproved of the deal. Maybe they thought she'd stop there to ask for help, or just get out of the snow."

"So what you're asking me to believe," he said, "is that the killer was at the parlor for a reason having nothing to do with them. That their showing up was a coincidence. Same as you and Carmen being there."

"*Rominichals suerte,*" she said with a grim smile. "It's a phrase my grandmother uses."

"Meaning . . . ?"

"Gypsy luck," she said.

Munch frowned and put some shrimp into the boiling kettle to cook.

"I still don't understand why you didn't tell me any of this before," he said.

"Carmen," she said. "I didn't want her being questioned by police or picked up by some child welfare agency. I thought if I could take her back to Washington, help her get away . . ." She shrugged. "I honestly hope this doesn't sound flip, but mistrust of authority's in my blood."

"And when you drove away from the *ofisa* . . . ?"

"I was bringing Carmen to the place where we've been staying. A friend's apartment," she said.

Munch looked at her and lifted his little basket of shrimp out of the broth.

"Suppose I go along with everything you've been telling me," he said, depositing the shrimp on his plate. "What about your father's claim that the Demetros did the killings? Is that also something I should discount?"

"I don't know," she said. "There's all that ancient history between Dad and Al Demetro. And there's Janos. If he got wind that Carmen was going to be more trouble than she was worth, he could have fallen back on his original demands for the money Dad owed. . . ."

She seemed about to say something more, but hesitated. Munch could see that opaque look coming into her eyes again, like a wall had dropped in front of them.

"What is it?" he said.

She stared at him in silence.

"Please," he said.

She kept staring at him.

"Vera," he said. "We have to trust each other." More silence.

He waited, appealing to her with his gaze.

"My father, he found a watch on the floor near Alexei and Christine," she said finally, expelling a long breath. "He told me about it yesterday, asked me not to say anything about it to the police. I promised him I wouldn't unless I had to. . . ."

"What is it that's important about the watch, Vera?"

"It had a broken band, and my father's positive it came off the killer's wrist when he was fighting with Alexei. And—"

"And . . . ?"

"There are engraved initials in the back plate of the watch," she said. "J.D."

Munch looked at her.

"Janos Demetro," he said.

"Apparently," she said.

TWELVE

SHE WASN'T SURE why she'd come back. Oh, there were all the reasons she'd given herself: the clothes she'd left behind, the few books and CDs, two or three photographs and sentimental items that she wanted to take with her. Nothing too heavy or too large, that was her rule; if it didn't fit into the box she'd brought along, it wasn't coming.

Carmen Bash stood in the foyer of the apartment where she'd lived for most of her fourteen years, buttoning her coat, the carton on the floor in front of her, filled up, taped shut, ready to go. Why had she really come back? If it had only been for her things, then why had she come *alone*? Vera would have gladly driven her in the Mustang, helped her pack, made it possible to bring away much more than she was physically able to lug onto a bus or train. Yet she hadn't even told her cousin of her plans, and had waited until she'd gone out with that detective to proceed with them.

She looked around, pulling up her collar, reaching into her pockets for her gloves. The place had never been much of anything: four cramped rooms, walls that needed painting, cockroaches in the kitchen sink, a ceiling that shook night and day from the parading feet of the kids upstairs. The windows in her room had looked down on an alley that ran along the back of the building, divided from the yard of a row house on the next street over by a low fence and ruled over by a vicious German shepherd. The dog was usually leashed to a post, but the shepherd always had enough freedom of movement to charge right up to the fence, and the slightest sound or stirring in the alley would make it agitated enough to bark and snarl and hurl itself against the chain link, smash into it again and again until it worked itself into a fury, growling, foaming, gnashing its teeth, pounding itself against the fence till blood was pouring from its snout. One day, when Vera was ten or eleven, she and one of the other girls who lived in the apartment building hadn't seen any sign of the dog and assumed its owner had brought it inside, and they were back there in the alley, bouncing a ball when it rolled through the space between the fence and the pavement and into the backyard of the row house. Vera's playmate reached for it on impulse and the dog appeared seemingly from out of nowhere, though Vera knew it must have been around the corner of the house, dozing at the end of its long line, and been disturbed by the rattling of the fence as the little girl stretched her hand out for the ball. It had rushed the fence in anger, loping like a wolf, its jaws opening and clamping down on the girl's hand before she could pull it back through to her side of the fence. The girl screamed—there was so much blood, blood covering her wrist, blood streaming between her fingers, blood all over the light summer shift she was wearing. . . .

In a way she'd been lucky, because her scream must have startled the shepherd for a split second, and given her a chance to pull her hand away before it was torn off. She'd gotten quite a few stitches where its teeth briefly sank into her arm, but was otherwise okay. And Vera had been even luckier, because she hadn't been the one to reach for the ball. And the dog, that dog must have had some good luck going for it too, because the police and ASPCA people that came to talk to its owner did not haul it off to the pound. Vera had heard that the owner was given a warning to keep the dog on a shorter leash, but to her knowledge he never did. Now, five years later, it was still lunging at anything that came near the fence. Except for a luckless cat or pigeon, though, it didn't wind up with much between its jaws. Everyone in Vera's building knew better than to go back there.

That monstrous creature was one of the many things Carmen had no regrets about leaving behind . . . like the hoop earrings and shawls and long Gypsy skirts her parents had forced her to wear on the days they'd kept her out of school to hand out flyers; like the flyers themselves, stacked on a shelf in what had been her parents' bedroom closet. Nor would she miss having to stand on a street corner and mouth the words her parents had made her repeat over and over as she passed out the flyers—*claravidente consejera,* clairvoyant consultations, spoken first in Romany, then in English— feeling so ashamed when she was seen by kids from school and their parents, feeling like a freak of nature, hating herself for being different, hating herself for letting her parents use her, hating herself, hating herself . . .

She blinked, her eyes beginning to sting. There wasn't much she'd miss about her old life; even its happier periods now seemed almost like medicine she'd been given to relieve the pain of a long and otherwise unbearable illness. For the most part these relative bright points had occurred during early childhood; her parents had laughed more then, and the extended family had often gathered in the living room, and her father had been very affectionate—although that had begun to change when the first swellings of her breasts became apparent under her clothes, as if he'd been frightened by her physical transformation. By the time she was thirteen, he'd come to ignore her altogether, leaving her to a mother who'd been preoccupied with earning money for the household, and instructing her in the *boojo,* the elaborate repertoire of stings and manipulations practiced upon marks by Gypsy women. . . .

No, there wasn't much about the past Carmen would miss, wasn't much that *deserved* to be missed . . . but hadn't she read that people who'd served prison sentences often felt lost when they were released, because after a while the bars and walls had gotten to be all they knew?

She had loved her parents.

Loved them in spite of everything.

She had loved them, and they were gone, dead and gone, and she was moving on toward a future that—like everyone else's—was unknown and unpredictable, opening out beyond the range of crystal balls, horoscopes, palm readings and tarot cards. And maybe she'd returned here to look back on who she'd been, so that she might better understand who she was becoming. . . .

But she'd taken long enough, and now it was time to go.

Tears burning hot tracks down her cheeks, Carmen lifted up the carton, wedged it into the crook of her arm, then pulled open the door with her free hand and left the home of her parents, and her childhood, behind forever.

"THERE SHE IS," Nino said.

He sat behind the steering wheel of Janos Demetro's black Lincoln, peering out the windshield as Carmen Bash pushed through the entry doors of 307 Belvedere Place and began walking across the courtyard toward the street.

"Pretty little filly," Kos said from the backseat. "Gonna be worth the wait."

"Shut up." Janos Demetro said, taking a drag of his cigarette. He was beside Nino in front. "Ain't no fucking way to talk."

Kos started to defend himself, but then his eyes met Janos's in the rearview and he thought the better of it.

For a moment the only sound in the car was the low whoosh of air from the heater vents.

"Better get ready, Kos," Nino said, fidgeting with the wheel, his fingers riding over the grips inside its rim. He was still watching the street with a kind of furtive impatience.

"You think I ain't?" Kos again. "I'm the one wanted to snatch her right when she got here."

"There was that guy out with his fucking dog," Nino said. "Last thing we need is some busybody making a commotion."

Silence except for the blowing heater.

Outside the car the renegade wind swayed bare trees and telephone wires, and spun braids of white powder from rooftop ledges. They were parked up the street from the apartment building, had been there when the girl arrived, waiting for her, as they had been waiting for days now. The lights of the sedan were doused, its windows tinted, and it sat at rest in the dark like a black manta awaiting easy prey.

The dash clock read nine o'clock.

"What's that she's carrying out?" Kos said.

"Looks like a box," said Nino.

"Her stuff," Janos said. "Be careful with it."

Kos grunted in acknowledgement and reached for the door handle.

"Kos . . ."

He glanced over the backrest at Janos.

"Careful with your piece too," Janos said.

She'd gotten to the sidewalk and turned left, heading for the bus stop on Thatcher, the same stop at which she'd arrived over an hour back. Another few steps and she would be passing the car.

Janos craned his head left, then right, scanning the street for bystanders. But it was night and the wind was blowing hard and the solid citizens were inside watching the tube.

"Okay," he said. "Do it."

Kos pushed out of the Lincoln as she came up to it, leaving his door halfway open. She turned toward him, saw him rushing toward her, and backed away with a startled expulsion of breath. She was holding the box close to her chest.

"Get in the car," he said in a near whisper.

He reached into his coat pocket with his right hand, then withdrew it just a little.

Just enough for Carmen to glimpse the pistol he was gripping.

She blinked in shock.

Kos reached back with his left hand and pulled open the car's rear door. Carmen glanced inside. There were two shadowy figures in front.

"I said get *in*," Kos rasped.

He let go of the door handle and stepped closer to Carmen, stepped *into* her, drawing his gun. She instinctively shoved the box against him, trying to ward him off, but it slipped from her grasp and fell to the pavement.

"Goddamn," he said, looking uncertainly down at it and remembering Janos's warning.

Suddenly the front passenger window went down a crack.

"Leave it now!" Janos hissed at him. "Just get a move on!"

Kos thrust his body against her, jamming the gun between them so she could feel its hardness against her stomach. His left hand gripped her elbow.

Paralyzed with fear and incomprehension, Carmen felt herself being pushed toward the car.

Kos moved behind her now, prodding her along with the nose of the gun.

Then she was shoved inside, shoved with such force that she spilled across the driveshaft hump, her face flat against the carpeting. Kos scrambled in after her and slammed the door shut.

"Let's go!" he said to Nino.

Nino popped the transmission into drive and the Lincoln glided away from the curb, stopping for a red light at the intersection, then turning right on the green, staying well below the speed limit as it joined the traffic heading toward the highway.

THIRTEEN

THE RINGING WOKE him at midnight.

Mihial Bash groped about in the darkness until his fingers made contact with the bedside phone. He'd been drinking before he fell asleep and the inside of his mouth was parched and sour.

"Who'zit," he mumbled foggily.

"Rise and shine," someone said in the earpiece.

The voice sounded familiar, but Mihial couldn't immediately place it. He pressed the button to light the face of his alarm clock and was taken aback by the lateness of the hour.

Who . . . ?

He jolted upright, his eyes opening wide, his body stiffening with tension as the caller's identity suddenly came to him.

"Janos?"

"Yeah."

"What do you wan—"

"Shut your mouth and pay attention," Janos said. "I picked up the girl tonight."

"Carmen? How the hell—"

"I told you to be quiet, old man," Janos said. "You want to deal here, we can deal."

Mihial heard a faint click in the receiver. Maybe Janos wasn't the only one on the line.

He swallowed dryly, his tongue thick in his mouth.

"Go ahead," he said.

"I'll take ten Gs for her."

"You got balls," Mihial said.

"That's my offer. It's good till tomorrow morning."

"Fucking balls. Your father know about this?"

"You better just worry about your own family," Janos said.

His anger a hot coal in his gut, Mihial thought about the revolver in the drawer of his nightstand.

"It's the middle of the night, you think I got ten thou at my fingertips?" His hand shook as he held the receiver to his ear. "And what you gonna do with Carmen if I don't?"

"Listen, I don't give a damn which way this goes," Janos said. "Either-or's fine by me. But I got places to send the kid. You don't pay and she's gone. Disappeared. Your choice."

"Look," Mihial said. He thought about his gun. "It's late, my head ain't even on straight yet. We can work this out."

"That a yes to my offer?" Janos said.

188

His tone was smug and mocking.

Mihial thought about his gun.

"Say where and when."

"Okay," Janos said. Practically grinning through the phone. "Okay, here it is. . . ."

IT WAS NEARLY one A.M. When Vera got back from her date with Munch, and as she tossed off her outer garments and put some water up to boil, thinking she'd have a cup of peppermint tea before turning in, she could not shake her surprise—make that *amazement*—over how well the night had gone.

And all things considered, it was amazing, wasn't it? Despite her misgivings about going out with a cop, despite having to delve into painful family conflicts and answer questions about the murder of Alexei and Christine, despite the mutual suspicion that had been a third party at their table, sitting between them throughout dinner like a rigid chaperone, despite every barrier, she'd gradually found herself loosening up for the first time since Carmen's phone call Sunday, and when Munch took the check and asked whether she wanted to stroll along the harbor she'd gladly said yes.

The trendy outlets on Pratt were open late for the holiday season, and leaving the Light Street Pavilion, Vera and Munch had joined the flow of shoppers walking past their nineteenth-century Expo facades, stopping now and then to look at the elaborate Christmas displays hurling a confetti of red and green light onto the snow-slick ground.

Walking east, they passed the World Trade Center and then ambled out on several of the piers like a couple of sightseers, huddling into their collars as the wind gusted in off the bay. They swung around the aquarium, and on Pier 3 stood looking out at the twinkling beacon of the Chesapeake lighthouse, and the old World War II coast guard cutter and submarine docked outside the Maritime Museum, and the tour boats rocking in the high, choppy waters. At some point they'd linked elbows and, their conversation easy and relaxed, headed back to the esplanade on Pratt Street, where they bought two coffees from an outdoor vendor, listened to a group of street musicians play rock versions of "Rudolph the Red-Nosed Reindeer" and "Jingle Bells" and watched a guy in a Santa suit juggle candy canes with glittery silver tassels. And after a while, as the crowds thinned and the night wore on toward a leisurely conclusion, they drifted north toward Lombard, and hailed a taxi, and Munch dropped her off at the condo that was presently her home away from home. When they got there, he leaned toward her ever so slightly, and gave her a chaste kiss on the lips before she reluctantly—and yes, she had to admit it, *breathlessly*—forced herself to draw away and say good night.

Now Vera rose from her chair at the kitchen table and hastened over to the stove, her thoughts interrupted by the fretful whistling of the teapot. The place had a single bedroom in which she and Carmen took turns sleeping, and though this was her designated night of exile on the living room couch, and the bedroom door was closed, she was afraid Carmen would be awakened by the piercing noise.

She lifted the kettle off the burner and filled her waiting cup with hot water, then carried it back to the table and sat down again, letting the tea bag steep. What exactly was it that attracted her to Munch? She supposed he *was* the most uncoplike cop she'd ever met, to use his own word. Beyond his obvious intelligence, and a kinetic sense of humor which had bounced from one association to another like a pinball firing off ringing, flashing bumpers, it was the complete absence of macho bluster in his personality that had caught her attention that first day in her father's apartment, and defied her expectations tonight. Throughout dinner Vera had waited for the square-jawed, reactive attitude she associated with lawmen to emerge, but it never had, even though he'd been very frank about having some serious questions for her, and relentless in his determination to get answers.

Vera sat there thinking and sipping her herbal tea, and had barely emptied half the cup when drowsiness began weighing down her eyelids. She glanced fuzzily up at the wall clock, saw that it was a quarter of two and decided to grab the paperback novel she'd been reading and hit the couch—and then suddenly realized her book was in the bedroom, along with the spare pillows and comforter reserved for whoever's turn it was on the couch.

She considered forgetting about all three, but it was much too chilly in the apartment to do without the quilt . . . and besides, she thought, Carmen wasn't a light sleeper, and probably wouldn't be disturbed if she crept in and out of the bedroom on her tiptoes.

Vera took off her shoes, got up and went to the bedroom. The crack under the door was dark, confirming that Carmen was asleep. No surprise there; it *was* two o'clock in the morning.

She turned the doorknob, eased the door partially open and slipped inside, pausing a moment to let her eyes adjust to the darkness. The chair with the pillows and folded blanket on it was to her right beside the bed. She took a step toward it—

And suddenly halted, icy darts shooting up and down her spine.

The bed.

The bed was empty.

"Carmen?" she said.

She gasped at the neatly made covers and fluffed pillows.

At a bed that obviously hadn't been slept in.

She looked around the room on impulse, her backbone a solid line of ice now, her heart bucking against her ribs. Looked around as if this might be some kind of prank and her niece might spring from behind the dresser like a cartoon ghost—*Boo! Here I am.* But that was absurd, that was the farthest thing from what she knew to be the truth.

She moved closer to the bed, helplessly reaching out to touch the unruffled blanket.

"Carmen," she repeated, her tone no longer questioning but clenched with fear.

Vera stood there in the dark for a moment that spooled out and out, fighting down panic, trying to stay rational, trying to think clearly about what to do.

Then, making up her mind, she turned and hurried out of the room.

STILL STAGGERING FROM a powerhouse one-two of nicotine withdrawal and sleep deprivation—the baby had been crying and filling her diapers all night because of an upset stomach—Pembleton nonetheless was his usual half hour early for work Thursday morning. Maybe his brain felt like a pincushion. Maybe his tongue felt like a sheet of aluminum foil. Maybe his eyes felt like live electrodes. There was no worse torment for him than wasting precious time.

After tossing his hat on the coat rack and getting a doughnut and cup of coffee, he sat at his desk and resumed doing the same thing he'd done to occupy himself while rubbing Olivia's tummy at two and three and four A.M.: thinking about his last visit to D'Angelo's bakeshop, which had left him with many more questions than it had answered.

What bothered him most was the fact that Tony D'Angelo had purposely kept his mother's involvement with the Bashes a secret when he was first interviewed. Even assuming his motive was nothing more than embarrassment over her having fallen prey to a Gypsy con, why continue dodging the subject *after* Francine herself had brought it out in the open? And why his sudden attitude change when Pembleton asked Francine the number of consultations she'd had with Christine Bash, and the extent to which her purse had been lightened as they progressed? Finally, what bearing, if any, did all this have on his murder investigation? After almost a week of chasing leads, very little about the Bash murders had gelled for him, and he couldn't shake the feeling that—

"Morning, pard."

He looked up from his coffee cup at Munch's smiling face.

"I assume you had a productive meeting with Vera Bash last night," Pembleton said.

"What makes you think that?" Munch asked.

"The grin on your kisser, for one thing," Pembleton said.

"*Kisser?*" Munch asked. "Interesting choice of words."

Pembleton shrugged. "George Raft used it in the movie I watched last night while I was up with Olivia."

"Yeah, but why not just say *face*?"

Pembleton shrugged again. "Variety."

"Or use a different synonym," Munch said. "Like *mug*, f'rinstance."

Pembleton wondered if there might be some

loophole in his nonsmoking pledge that would allow him to light up just *once* before the day was over.

"Munch, what's this about—"

"I think you were trying to imply something," Munch said, unbuttoning his coat.

"All I asked—"

"Was whether I got anywhere with Vera Bash," Munch said. "A loaded question, don't you think?"

"Now *you're* the one who's playing with words," Pembleton said, thinking that he had maybe thirty seconds before he blew his cool.

"So tell me," Munch said. "Would you describe my smile as puckish or effervescent?"

"I got better ways of describing it, my man."

They both glanced over at Detective Meldrake Lewis, who had moseyed over to Pembleton's desk after entering the squad room. A bearded, compact black man in his middle thirties, Lewis had grappled his way out of the projects to become one of the best cops on the squad. Regarded by many as a kind of street-smart knight, he walked the walk, talked the talk and wore his tough ghetto background like a suit of armor.

"Oh yeah?" Munch said.

"Yeah," Lewis said. "It's the kinda smile a guy wears when he's been playin' elevator."

" 'Playing elevator'?"

"Poundin' the hammer."

"Huh?" Munch said.

"Bein' halfa the double-backed beast."

Munch cocked an eyebrow.

"Gettin' some," Lewis said, and bopped off to the coffee room.

Munch sighed and looked at Pembleton.

"Getting back to our case—" he said.

As if I'm the one who got us *off* the subject, Pembleton thought.

"I *did* make some progress with Vera yesterday."

"So fill me in."

Munch pulled a chair up to Pembleton's desk, turned it around, straddled it backward and filled Pembleton in, summarizing Vera's explanation of what she was doing at the *ofisa* Monday morning, and concluding with what she'd told him about the watch Mihial had found.

"And her story's got you hooked?" Pembleton said.

"She didn't have anything to do with the shootings," Munch said. "Trust me."

Pembleton looked at him.

"Trust you," he said.

"Right."

"Like I'm already trusting you about going cold turkey."

"Exactly."

Pembleton frowned with exasperation. "What I'd like to know, oh wise and beneficient Oz, is when this 'trust and faith' thing between us is going to start working my way."

"The time will come," Munch said sagely, his arms folded on the shoulder rest of the chair.

Pembleton sighed, reached into his in-box and began checking his messages. There had been a call from a guy named David King relating to a case he and Bayliss had been working for the past six months, a call from a West Coast manufacturer of children's furniture that he'd contacted regarding their supposedly innovative playpens, a call from an ADA who was prosecuting one of Pembleton's recent collars. . . .

"We'd better get hold of that watch," he said, and for no ascribable reason found himself thinking about the D'Angelos. "While we're at it, we'd also better see if there's any new info from the lab. . . ."

He let the sentence trail off, suddenly preoccupied, unable to shake off the questions that had been troubling him since yesterday. Nor were they all of it. There was something else, a thought that had scampered across the back of his head like a rodent had left its hole only long enough to tantalize him with its presence, and then popped out of sight when he tried to snare it.

"How'd your follow-up at the bakery go?" Munch said, as if having read his mind.

"It—"

Frank broke off again.

He stared absently at the little piece of paper in his hand. Stared at the "From" line without actually reading the name that was written on it. Stared at it and flashed back to his conversation with Francine D'Angelo.

You have to understand, this only started after Jack passed away.

Jack?

My husband.

"Hey, Frank," Munch said. "You with me?"

Pembleton looked at the memo sheet in his hand. What he saw in the space for the caller's name was not the one that had been written there by whoever took the message, but another name . . . a name that seemed to pulse before his eyes in big, three-dimensional block letters.

"J.D." Pembleton said, thinking aloud. "The initials on the back of the watch—"

"Yeah?" Munch said.

"Maybe it didn't belong to Al Demetro's son Janos," Pembleton said, thinking aloud. "Maybe it belonged to Tony D'Angelo's *father*."

"Frank, no offense, but I don't know what the hell you're saying."

"I'm not sure I do, either," Pembleton said. "But when I was at the bakery the day of the murders . . . the kid, Tony . . . he looked down at his wrist to check the time and . . ."

Anything wrong?

Must've forgotten my watch.

Munch heard the phone on his desk ringing and motioned for Lewis to answer for him.

"And *what*?" he said to Pembleton.

"He—"

"Yo, Munchkin!" Lewis called across the room, holding up Munch's phone.

198

"Do me a favor and take a message," Munch said.

"Be a *fe*male, says it's urgent." Lewis put his hand over the bottom of the receiver and winked. "Probably that number you took out last night. Can't get *enough* of you."

Munch cocked an eyebrow. "I'll take it over here."

Pembleton shoved his phone across to Munch, who lifted the receiver and punched up his extension.

"Hello?" he said, and paused to listen.

Pembleton waited.

"*What?*" Munch said into the receiver. He listened some more, his face suddenly becoming grave.

"Stay put, I'm on my way," he said, then hung up and sprang off his seat so suddenly it almost toppled over.

"Let's go," he said to Frank.

"Go *where*?" Pembleton said. "Who was that on the phone?"

"Vera Bash," Munch said hurriedly. "Carmen's missing. We have to get to the *ofisa*."

He turned and went racing out of the squad room.

A split second later Pembleton grabbed his coat and followed him out the door.

FOURTEEN

"WHERE DO YOU think your father will be meeting Janos?" Pembleton asked.

He and Munch were standing with Vera Bash in the apartment above the *ofisa*, which they had reached by car after a fifteen-minute shot through heavy rush-hour traffic, their flashing bubble light and blaring siren clearing the road ahead of them.

Vera looked around as if the answer to his question might be hidden somewhere in the room, perhaps behind a piece of furniture or a wall hanging.

"I don't know," she said at last, utter futility in her tone. "I just don't know."

Munch regarded her silently.

"How long's it been since Mihial left?" he asked after several seconds had lapsed.

"He was heading out the door when I phoned you," she said. Her eyes were red from crying and lack of sleep. "I tried to get him to stay, but he wouldn't listen. . . ."

Vera shook her head again. When the detectives had arrived minutes earlier, she had quickly told them what had happened since she'd walked into the bedroom last night and realized Carmen was gone. Soon after making her discovery, she'd driven over to Belvedere Court in her Mustang, partly because she remembered Carmen having once mentioned she wanted to go back for some of her things, and partly because she didn't know where else to start looking for her. Vera knocked on the door of Carmen's old apartment for quite a while before abandoning hope that she was there, and as she left the building she stumbled upon the cardboard box lying on the street, and recognized a number of Carmen's belongings in the spill of odds and ends on the sidewalk around it. That was when she rushed over to her father's place in desperation and was told about Janos's ultimatum—although Mihial refused to let her know how much cash Janos was demanding in exchange for Carmen, or where and when it was to be delivered. By then, she told the detectives, it must have been something like four in the morning, and she had called the precinct twice, on both instances leaving messages for Munch—messages which were presumably still on his desk, mixed in with all the others that he hadn't had a chance to read before Vera telephoned a third time, and finally reached him.

"Did your father say anything when he walked

out, besides telling you he was going to bring back Carmen?" Munch asked her now.

She shook her head. "Only that he'd be finished with the Demetros when this was over, and didn't want me getting in his way."

"What do you think he meant by 'finished'?"

"I have no idea," she said. "But if you'd seen how he was acting before he left . . . I'm afraid that he's up to something crazy."

"Is it possible he's armed?"

"I don't know," she said. "I'm not even sure whether he *owns* a gun."

Munch turned to Pembleton.

"You suppose they could be making the swap at Al Demetro's clubhouse?" he asked.

"If I were Janos, I wouldn't do it there," Pembleton said. "Even if his old man knows about this, he'd never approve."

"What about at one of the Demetros' fortune-telling joints?"

"Their clan must run a dozen *ofisas* in this city," Vera said. "How are you going to search all of them in time?"

"We'll have to open this up wide, bring in some extra manpower," Pembleton said. "If Janos has kidnapped Carmen, then the situation's escalated beyond anything we can handle ourselves."

"Are you saying you intend to put out some kind of general alert? Get the whole police department involved?"

"There doesn't seem to be any alternative," Pembleton said.

"For God's sake, don't you see we'll *lose* Carmen that way?" she said. "If Janos gets wind that you're coming after him, he'll have her moved out of the city. You have to recognize that the Gypsy community is still basically nomadic. The people that took Carmen probably have all kinds of false identification, friends and relatives in other states. . . . They can slip out of town at a moment's notice."

"Vera, listen," Munch said. "We can't just wait around here until—"

"Tsatshimo tomenge patshivalo."

All three of them turned toward the entryway, where Betshi Bash, Vera's grandmother, had suddenly appeared from her bedroom. All skin and bones, she had on slippers and a loose robe, the sash of which was drawn tight around her withered frame.

Munch glanced at Vera. "What did she say?"

"The truth . . . is a gift reserved for the worthy," Vera said, bewildered. "It's another one of her proverbs. I-I don't know what she means. . . ."

Betshi Bash shuffled forward a little and looked directly at Munch, her eyes gleaming in her lined, gray face.

"I have phone in my room, listen when Janos call," she said in broken English. "Hear all he say."

"Why didn't you tell us sooner—"

"Shhhh, no time now!" she said, holding up a

bony finger. "I never in my life talk to *gajo*. But Vera trust you, so I must too."

Munch stared at her.

"Go on," he said, swallowing. "Please."

She shuffled closer to Munch, leaning in toward him, putting her lips to his ear. Her breath felt dry as ashes against his face.

"I tell you where my son go," she whispered. "Tell you where they bring Carmen."

THE SWAP WAS to occur at nine A.M. sharp on Pier 14, one of the many rotting, neglected wharves southeast of Inner Harbor. Mihial knew it was a perfect place for a setup, but the whole thing had been laid out for him right off, and he'd been in no position to argue.

That was okay, though.

He had a surprise of his own in store for Janos.

Mihial checked his wristwatch. Eight-forty-five. He had begun to sweat from sheer nerves and was getting chilled. The waiting was enough to drive him out of his mind.

Stamping his feet, blowing cigarette smoke into the icy morning air, Mihial retraced steps he'd taken dozens of times in the last hour. The L-shaped wharf was deserted from one end to the other and he paced restlessly in the shadow of the abandoned marine firehouse on his right, squatting there at the water's edge like a sullen old man who clings to a neighborhood many years after its decline. He walked out along the disintegrating planks, reached a point where they suddenly gapped over the water, and then turned back toward shore, trying to avoid the mounds of rubbish that formed an obstacle course around him. Strong offshore winds had kept the wharf from getting its fair share of snow, whipping up and scattering the flakes before they could settle over the yellowed scraps of newspaper, junk-food wrappers, broken wine and beer bottles, tires, packing crates, syringes and used condoms that littered its narrow length.

Mihial paced and smoked. The wind clawed at him. His head ached from all the drinking he'd done the night before. He accidentally kicked a bottle and jumped a little, startled, his breath catching as the bottle clinked away from his shoe.

The waiting.

The damned waiting.

He did not know how much longer he could stand it.

He finished his cigarette, snapped it into the water and glanced at his watch again. Only five minutes had passed, passed with agonizing slowness, curling and wilting and falling away like petals from a drying flower.

Except for a group of sea gulls bobbing in the currents off the pier, he was still alone.

Mihial turned from the water, walked to the long-unused parking area at the head of the pier and paused to observe the crosstown traffic artery running past it. He had no doubt Janos would arrive by that route. It was the most direct one from the west side.

He looked on as a big semi rumbled by, followed in rapid succession by a small foreign hatchback and a Chevy Corsica. Then the road was empty awhile and everything was very quiet.

The wind blew. Water lapped at the piles. The gulls didn't move. Eight-fifty-five, nine o'clock.

Mihial paced a couple of steps one way, then the other, watching the road.

Soon he saw another car approaching in the eastbound lane. A Lincoln Continental, the right make and model. Its engine was almost soundless and the sunlight made eel-slippery reflections on its buffed black finish.

He watched with tense anticipation as it swung into the parking area and stopped on the hot top some yards from him.

Several minutes crept by.

Mihial felt his stomach tighten.

Finally a large man in a leather jacket and floppy wide-brimmed hat stepped out of the driver's door. He was joined a moment later by a smaller man who exited from the passenger side. They stood in front of the idling Continental, facing Mihial in silence. Then the one with the floppy hat went around to the rear and pulled open a third door.

An instant later Janos emerged. His hair was slicked back and he was wearing mirrored aviator glasses and a dark overcoat. He looked at Mihial and smiled and then reached a hand into the car.

Mihial had just enough time to realize he was tugging at someone's arm before Carmen stumbled out, her heels scraping on the blacktop.

Janos pulled her up against him, keeping his hand locked around her elbow. His two bodyguards waited on either side of the car like bookends.

"*Yekka Romanish,*" he said, giving Mihial the traditional Gypsy greeting.

Still grinning like a shark.

Mihial nodded slowly but said nothing.

Janos drew Carmen closer to him and smoothed a hand over her dark hair.

"*May kali I muri may gugli avela,*" he said in Romany.

The darker the berry, the sweeter it is.

There was an implicit leer in his tone.

Mihial thought about the gun in his coat pocket.

"So this is what it's come to," he said. "Look at you. Acting like a *gaje* criminal."

"Say anything you want, old man," Janos said. "I'm here. You're here. After all these years you're gonna settle up with my family, and it wasn't my father or the *baro* who got you to do it. It was me."

Mihial thought about the gun, forcing himself not to reach for it

Not yet.

"Yeah, Janos," he said. "It's you for sure."

"THIS IS A police emergency; move your vehicles to one side!" Pembleton's voice boomed from the horn, many times amplified. "I said *move* it!"

The Honda up ahead swung to the right and out of the way, while the passenger van in front of it swung left, leaving a stretch of the middle lane clear form Munch and Pembleton.

"You're like Moses parting the Red Sea," Munch said, raising his voice above the howl of the siren.

Pembleton lowered the mike from his face. "That make Fell's Point the promised land?"

Munch smiled bleakly.

They were speeding down Broadway in their unmarked Plymouth, racing the clock as it ticked closer to nine A.M., which was when the dockside meeting between Mihial Bash and Janos Demetro was supposed to come off.

Neither man was optimistic about their prospects of reaching the harbor on time. It was just shy of eight-fifty, and they were not only coming from the opposite side of town, but still had several miles to travel through heavy traffic. Also, while they had radioed for assistance and were expecting squad cars from the local precinct at the scene, the thought of being johnny-come-latelies was making both detectives jumpy.

Now the dispatcher's voice crackled over the radio, confirming that several patrol units would indeed be responding to their call.

"It relieve you knowing those uniforms'll be there?" Munch said.

"To no end," Pembleton said.

He looked out the windshield, noticed a large commercial van rattling along about three or four

209

car lengths ahead of them and snatched the microphone off the clip again.

"*Out of the lane! Let's go!*" he shouted, stomping down on the gas pedal. "*Move, move, move, move, move!*"

Yeah, Munch thought.

Definitely relieved to no end.

"ENOUGH BULLSHIT," JANOS said. "Let's you and me get this over with."

Mihial nodded. He could hear the wind blasting over the harbor, and the lapping of the oily water against the dock.

"I got the money in here," he said bitterly, extending his duffel to Janos. "You can open it and see for yourself."

"Put the bag down on the ground," Janos snapped, the sun flashing off his mirrored lenses, his tone full of arrogance and contempt, just as it had been on the phone the night before.

Mihial looked at him, wishing he could see his eyes. You could read a lot about a man's intentions in his eyes.

He set the bag down in front of himself.

"Okay," he said, and took a deep breath. "Now let's see you live up to your end of the bargain."

Janos stood silently a moment. Then he nodded and let go of Carmen's arm.

"Take off," he said to her.

At first she didn't move, didn't even seem to understand him. Just stood there, her face streaked from dried-up tears, her eyes glazed over, her long black hair in tangled disarray. It was as if her mind had reacted to the strains of her ordeal by sealing her in a kind of protective bubble.

"I told you get outta here," Janos said impatiently.

This time the harshness of his tone got through to her. She actually started, like someone suddenly awakened from a deep sleep.

She stepped weakly away from Janos, her stride a little off balance, then stopped and turned to her uncle.

"Uncle Mihial?" she said. "Are you coming with me?"

"Go," he said, gesturing toward the street behind the pier.

She stared at him, her face pale, fresh tears spilling from her eyes.

"But—"

"Go home," Mihial said.

Smiling gently.

She hesitated another moment, the wind whipping her hair about her shoulders, looking small and afraid in the cold sunlight of the near-winter morning.

Then she nodded and walked quickly past him. He snapped his head over his shoulder, watched her move across the lot and then stop to look at him once she'd reached the bordering sidewalk.

He motioned for her to keep going and she reluctantly turned and walked away.

"You can relax. We won't come after her again."

Mihial turned suddenly, saw that Janos had moved closer to him. His thugs were still bracketing the Lincoln's front grille.

Each of them had slid a gun from underneath his coat and was pointing it in his direction.

"What the hell is this?" Mihial said. "I brought the cash—"

"You think I'm going to *deal* with a nobody like you?" Janos said, taking off his sunglasses and dropping them into his pocket.

He walked up to Mihial, glared at him a second, then looked down at the satchel and violently kicked it aside.

"I don't give a *shit* about your money!" he said. Something profoundly hateful was boiling up in him, breaking through is stony composure. "You owed my family for years and we let you slide. And what did you do to show your fucking gratitude? You bad-mouthed us. Tried pinning those *murders* on us."

"Tell me I'm wrong," Mihial said contemptuously. "Like it wasn't your watch I found."

Janos looked at him.

"I don't know what you're talking about."

"Sure you don't." Mihial angrily jabbed his chin toward the Lincoln. "And maybe that wasn't the car I saw outside my *ofisa* after you chucked a Molotov cocktail through the window."

"The fire wouldn't have happened if you hadn't started this whole thing," Janos said. "My father

212

should've taken care of you a long time ago. But he wasn't strong enough. So now I got to do it."

"You?" Mihial said. "You're just a bug compared to Al."

Janos's eyes bulged. His breath was coming hard.

"A fucking bug," Mihial said, provoking him.

His lips twisted with rage, Janos shoved a hand into his coat pocket. When he brought it out a pulse beat later, Mihial saw something bright slice upward in front of them, and instantly knew Janos was gripping a knife.

Janos stood there sucking down air in febrile gasps, the blade gleaming in his fist like a steel talon.

"You know what kind of knife this is," he said.

It wasn't a question.

Mihial stared at the wavy, double-edged blade. "A *kris*," he said. Recognizing the traditional instrument of Rom justice. "It still don't make you the man your father is."

He nodded to indicate the two gunnies by the car.

"Neither do they," he said.

His eyes meeting Janos's eyes.

Holding them.

Communicating that he wasn't afraid, even as he slipped a hand into his own pocket.

"Maggot," he said.

Janos lunged at him then, his temper reaching its flashpoint, his knife a glittering ripple of motion. The inarticulate growl of fury that tore from his throat was almost bestial.

Mihial backstepped out of the weapon's deadly trajectory, whipping the little snub-nosed revolver out of his pocket, holding it out between Janos and himself.

"Now, punk," he said, and cocked back the hammer of the gun. He could feel his heart pounding, feel blood surging up to the roof of his skull. "Now we're gonna see justice—"

He suddenly fell silent, his throat locking around rest of the sentence.

Inches in front of him, Janos tilted his head a little to one side, listening, sweat pouring down his brow.

Both of them stood motionless, the scream of approaching police sirens growing louder and louder around them.

MUNCH AND PEMBLETON were clipping along the access road to the docks when Munch looked out his window and spotted the Lincoln pulling out of the lot up ahead. Twisting around in his seat, he tapped Pembleton's arm and pointed to the vanity tag on its front bumper: "Demetro."

Pembleton floored the accelerator and the Plymouth jolted forward. Outside their windows the air throbbed with the ululating scream of police sirens as their backup units converged on the scene.

Wheeoooowheeeeeooewheeeeoooooooooooo—

The Plymouth surged toward Pier 14, its tires spinning up ice and snow, bits of crumbled road tar

214

dinging against its chassis as it bumped over craters that would have looked at home on the moon.

The detectives screeched to a halt across the front of the Lincoln, blocking it from the roadway. Munch saw the black sedan suddenly kick into reverse, then cut sharply to the right.

"Shit!" He motioned toward the fence surrounding the lot on three sides. "They're going right through the chain-link!"

His face tight with concentration, Pembleton wrenched the wheel to the left, simultaneously stepping on the gas. The Plymouth swung into a ninety-degree turn and went bumping into the parking area. Keeping his foot down on the gas, Pembleton raced up alongside the fugitive Lincoln, overtook it and once again came to an abrupt, pebble-and-ice-spitting stop across its path.

"Shit!" Munch yelled again, gripping the strap above the passenger door and bracing for a collision. But the Lincoln veered off to the left, its front end avoiding the Plymouth's flank, then slid erratically from side to side for several yards before its driver hit the brakes.

"Stay where you are—police!" Pembleton shouted into the horn. He heard sirens up close, glanced in the rearview and saw two teams of blues arriving in their radio cars, one pulling into the lot behind the other.

Munch was drawing his service pistol even as he shouldered open his door and jumped outside. He ran toward the Lincoln and stopped less than a yard from its passenger door, his legs spread wide, holding his gun straight out with both hands.

"Get out!" he shouted at the top of his voice. "Now!"

Nothing happened.

"I said *now*, goddamn it!"

His heart pounding, the metallic taste of adrenaline filling his mouth, Munch stood there with his knuckles white around the butt of his gun, half expecting to be slammed off his feet by a volley of slugs.

Finally a passenger door swung open.

Then the driver's door.

Munch held his breath and waited.

He immediately recognized the men who exited the car—their hands raised above their heads in surrender—as the pair of checker players from Al Demetro's clubhouse.

"Turn around and put your hands on the hood of the car! Both of you!" he shouted, motioning with his gun. Out the corner of his eye he spotted Pembleton running up beside him, his own weapon at the ready. "Don't get any ideas!"

They assumed the position like seasoned pros.

The detectives patted them down, found a gun in each of their jackets, plus a third pistol strapped to the ankle of the guy with the Bucharest flop hat.

"The girl's okay. We didn't do anything to her," he said as Munch cuffed him.

"Those two nutjobs went and offed each other,"

the other thug told Pembleton. "Settled their fucking feud."

Pembleton and Munch exchanged looks behind their backs. But the question on the minds of both detectives was answered before either could voice it.

"You guys better come and see this," one of the blues said, trotting over from the far end of the lot. "We got a couple of fresh ones over by the pier."

AS THE DETECTIVES had immediately suspected, the bodies—found sprawled on the frozen tar mere inches from one another—were those of Mihial Bash and Janos Demetro.

Bash had been stabbed to death. The knife that had killed him was sunk deep in his rib cage after having been driven into his belly and slitting him open from there on up. Looking down at him, Munch could see grayish intestinal coils protruding between the flaps of his jacket. The snubby bore of the .38 in his lifeless grip was still warm.

Demetro had been shot to death. The holes blown into his chest by Mihial's pistol were somewhat neater than the wounds he'd inflicted on Mihial with his *kris,* but what really counted was the end result, which was of course the same for both men.

Their steaming blood had mingled between them on the blacktop, and Munch couldn't help thinking that was perversely symbolic of what the thug named Kos had said when he'd been frisked outside the Lincoln: the feud was over.

He gazed across the parking lot to where Carmen Bash sat hunched and weeping in the backseat of a patrol car. One of the blues had picked her up several blocks away.

"Poor kid," Munch said. He thought about everything she'd been through, thought about having to tell Vera her father was dead . . . and then tried not to think at all.

Pembleton made a low, indeterminate sound in his throat. He had slipped on a protective latex glove, knelt down beside Mihial's corpse and gotten busy fishing around in his pockets.

"Find anything?" Munch said when he finally rose from the body.

"Only this," Pembleton said, holding out his hand so Munch could see the watch he'd taken from Bash's trouser pocket.

Pembleton briefly inspected the watch's broken band, then turned it facedown in his palm. The inscribed initials in back looked almost molten in the hard bright sunlight.

J.D.

"You think that'll help us nail whoever did Alexei and Christine?" Munch said.

Pembleton looked at him.

"Time will tell," he said.

FIFTEEN

AS IT TURNED out, Pembleton and Munch didn't need the watch—or any other piece of evidence—to help them nail their murderer. On Monday morning, almost one week to the hour after the start of their investigation into the deaths of Christine and Alexei Bash, they got something that any dutiful murder cop would consider a gift greater than money, jewels or even an expenses paid trip to Rio with first class accommodations all the way: a full and voluntary confession from the killer.

What made this particular confession out of the ordinary was that it literally came straight to their door, delivered by a gaunt and guilt-ridden Tony D'Angelo, whose first words to Pembleton as he strode over to his desk were "I killed those two people, and I guess I'll have to pay, but they shouldn't've messed with my mom, y'know?"

Pembleton thought maybe he did know, or at least had a pretty good notion, one that was confirmed to both him and Munch fifty minutes later in the unsparing white light of the square, brick-walled interrogation room referred to around the station as the Box.

In this instance Pembleton did it strictly by the book. After reciting Miranda-Escovedo to the kid, and having him waive his right to an attorney, and seating him in the presence of a police stenographer, an ADA and a tripod-mounted video camera—not to mention Munch and himself—he asked him to please give his name, date of birth and current address, then slid his chair up close to D'Angelo, looked him squarely in the eye and invited him to unburden his conscience.

"Start at the beginning," he said.

And so the kid did, in a long but remarkably coherent monologue, telling the cops of the day Christine Bash first approached his mother about coming into the fortune-telling parlor for a consultation. . . .

"This wasn't a week after my father was buried, and Mom was really falling apart. . . ."

Falling apart and vulnerable and desperately in need of spiritual reassurance, a need which Christine had readily exploited. She had been very delicate and sympathetic in her approach, offering Mrs. D'Angelo at least one session as a neighborly kindness, without fee or obligation, just come in and see if you feel any better afterward, why don't you? Soon after that initial pitch, Tony's mother had taken Christine up on her offer, and been amazed by her insight into the pain and doubt she'd been feeling since her husband's death, and by the way she'd known so many details about her personal life.

"Mom got hooked right off," Tony explained. "I mean she started going back to that Gypsy joint maybe once a week, then twice. . . ."

And pretty soon she became consumed by her visits, always talking about Christine's sensitivity and powers, returning home with all sorts of occult paraphernalia—crystals, charms, candles, incense, potions, you name it. After a month or so she was going for consultations almost daily and refusing to answer Tony's questions about how much she was spending, though he knew it must have been a lot, because the bakery's suppliers were calling about unpaid bills, threatening to halt deliveries unless their accounts were evened up.

"Right away that got me thinking. See, I'm at the place every day, and I know business was the same as usual, and that we never had cash problems before she got involved with the Gypsy woman's hocus-pocus. . . ."

Francine D'Angelo's behavior reached its "peak of weirdness," as Tony put it, on the six-month anniversary of her husband's death. It was a Sunday morning in October, the bakery closed, both Tony and Francine spending the day at home, and he vividly remembered walking in on her as she was writing a check at the dining room table, catching her by surprise because she'd thought he was working on his car in the garage—which he had been, except he'd cut his finger and gone inside for a Band-Aid. If it hadn't been for the nervous, guarded look on her face, he might not have gotten curious at that particular moment, and gone over to the table, and seen that her check was being made out for the sum of four thousand dollars, payable to Cash.

"Right off, even before I ask her anything about it, she starts coming up with excuses for why she's emptying out one of the bank accounts," the kid told the detectives. "Like, she told me she was withdrawing the money to pay off some of the bills, which didn't make sense. I know how our business runs, and we never pay for *anything* in cash. If that'd been what she was doing, she would've been writing checks to the people we *owed*. The whole thing got me real suspicious. . . ."

So suspicious, in fact, that he asked her point-blank if the money was going to her fortune-teller. Though she hemmed and hawed a little, he knew by her reaction that he'd hit on the truth, and kept pressing her until she finally admitted it. What he learned was that Christine Bash had convinced her that Jack's spirit was in a state of unrest, that this was due to her family's luck having been crossed in some way, and that to remove the evil influences and set things right, certain Gypsy bishops would have to participate in the magical work Christine was doing . . . bishops who would need to be paid cash down in exchange for their time.

222

Tony had scarcely been able to believe what he'd heard from his mother's lips that day, it had all been so crazy, but there was nothing he could say to dissuade her from giving the fortune-teller the four thousand. It hadn't even mattered when he got angry, and told her how he couldn't believe she was throwing money out the window at a time when their growing debt had put them in danger of losing the business his father had worked so hard to build up.

That very day, Tony started thinking he needed to take matters in hand. He was still wrestling with the question of how a couple of weeks later when his mother unwittingly answered it for him. They were in the bakery at the time, his mother having just returned from one of her readings in a state Tony described to Munch and Pembleton as one of great concern. When Tony asked her what was wrong, she told him she'd seen Christine place a considerable sum of money in a small floor safe behind the parlor, and had warned Christine that it wasn't a good idea keeping it in there, that those safes were notoriously insecure and could easily be carried off by a burglar. . . .

"Imagine, that witch is squeezing my mother dry, and meanwhile mom's giving *her* advice about how to keep from being ripped off," Tony explained, the recollection making him visibly agitated. "It was too fucking much. Soon as I heard about the Mickey Mouse safe those Gypsies were using, I decided to break into their place and rob them. Like they'd

223

been robbing my mother, making a *fool* outta her, for more than half a year. . . ."

Once Tony decided on his course of action, nothing could have changed his mind, and he spent the next few weeks getting ready, watching the Bashes' storefront, keeping track of their comings and goings. The tools he figured he'd need for the theft were nothing special, since the Gypsies didn't even have an insurance gate or burglar alarm. A crowbar to pry open the door, a hacksaw to cut the safe, one or two other items—he'd purchased all of them right at the hardware store on his block.

The gun, of all things, was really an afterthought. Tony picked it up on the street just days before he finally went ahead with the job, figuring he should have some protection in the event someone walked in on him . . . which, in the end, was precisely— and tragically—what happened.

"When Christine and her husband showed up, I just sort of lost it," Tony said, shaking his head as he concluded his story. "I never meant to kill anybody, but they were fucking crooks . . . *Gypsies*. How was I supposed to know what they'd do to me? How was I supposed to *know?*"

"And why'd you decide to come in and tell us this?" Pembleton asked.

"It was that story in the paper about those two who killed each other, Mihial and that other guy. Demetrius, or whatever. About how there was bad blood between them because of what happened to Christine and her husband, and how Mihial blamed the other guy for it. I just couldn't go on feeling guilty. Knowing it was my fault."

He was silent a moment, and then his shoulders clenched up and the inevitable tears started to fall.

"No matter how much I hated those people, I couldn't go on like that," the kid snuffled into his hands.

Pembleton looked at him, released a long, weary sigh and reached over to turn off the video camera.

Confession over, case closed.

"ONE CASE, ONE arrest," Bayliss was saying to Pembleton. "I'd say you and Munchkin had a pretty good week."

It was an hour after they'd booked Tony D'Angelo for second-degree murder and lesser charges relating to his robbery of the *ofisa* (by his own admission there had been about two thousand dollars in the safe he'd carried away), and with Bayliss back on his regular schedule and seated across from Pembleton, things were feeling back to normal in the squad room . . . at least as normal as things *ever* felt for men and women whose days were spent hunting down killers.

"Oh, it was fabulous," Pembleton said. He was staring at the pack of cigarettes on his desk, debating whether or not to have a smoke. And why not? His season in hell with Munch was over; he was free of his vow. "Yes, indeed. A fabulous, marvelous week."

"You being sarcastic, Frank?"

225

"Me?" Pembleton put a hand on his chest. "What gives you that impression?"

Bayliss pulled a face.

"I like you better when you're sucking on butts," he said, nodding toward Pembleton's cigarettes. "No pun intended."

Pembleton gave him an ornery grin, and was about to tackle some paperwork when he noticed Munch putting on his coat. He set down the file folder in his hand, rose quickly from his chair and caught up to him just as he was walking out the door.

"Mihial's funeral's today, isn't it?" he asked.

"That's where I'm headed," Munch said, nodding.

"Meeting Vera?"

"Yeah," Munch said. "Some second date."

They looked at each other a moment.

"I keep thinking that Mihial and Janos still might be alive if the kid had come down with the guilts a few days sooner," Munch said. "If Mihial had known Janos didn't kill Alexei and Christine, he might not have gone off the way he did. . . ."

"If, maybe," Pembleton said. "They're words I never worry about."

Munch sighed.

"Guess we should chalk it up to Gypsy luck," he said, and unexpectedly extended his hand for Pembleton to shake.

Pembleton reached out and grasped it firmly.

"See you later," Munch said.

"Later," Pembleton said.

He stood by the door for several seconds looking after Munch as he turned into the hallway.

Then he remembered the stack of open case files waiting on his desk, and went back to work.